"Make the most of it, lady,"

Jeff challenged. "Put on your flashiest dress and come with me to the yacht club party on Saturday."

Kate had sensed what was coming. All the same, she felt her stomach clench. "Jeff, it's not that simple," she muttered. "I can't just—"

"Come on. Yes, you can," Jeff urged.

"But what about all those people? What about your mother, for heaven's sake? I know what she thinks of me."

"Kate, don't let these people intimidate you," he said.

"I'm not intimidated. Not by anyone."

"Then prove it. Because when I walk into that place with you on my arm," Jeff went on, "lady, we're going to knock their socks off!"

Dear Reader,

This month, Silhouette Romance has six irresistible, emotional and heartwarming love stories for you, starting with our FABULOUS FATHERS title, *Wanted: One Son* by Laurie Paige. Deputy sheriff Nick Dorelli had watched the woman he loved marry another and have that man's child. But now, mother and child need Nick. Next is *The Bride Price* by bestselling author Suzanne Carey. Kyra Martin has fuzzy memories of having just married her Navajo ex-fiancé in a traditional wedding ceremony. And when she discovers she's expecting his child, she knows her dream was not only real...but had mysteriously come true! We also have two not-to-be missed new miniseries starting this month, beginning with *Miss Prim's Untamable Cowboy*, book 1 of THE BRUBAKER BRIDES by Carolyn Zane. A prim image consultant tries to tame a very masculine working-class wrangler into the true Texas millionaire tycoon he really is. Good luck, Miss Prim!

In *Only Bachelors Need Apply* by Charlotte Maclay, a man-shy woman's handsome new neighbor has some secrets that will make her the happiest woman in the world, and in *The Tycoon and the Townie* by Elizabeth Lane, a struggling waitress from the wrong side of the tracks is romanced by a handsome, wealthy bachelor. Finally, our other new miniseries, ROYAL WEDDINGS by Lisa Kaye Laurel. The lovely caretaker of a royal castle finds herself a prince's bride-to-be during a ball...with high hopes for happily ever after in *The Prince's Bride*.

I hope you enjoy all six of Silhouette Romance's terrific novels this month...and every month.

Regards,

Melissa Senate,
Senior Editor

Please address questions and book requests to:
Silhouette Reader Service
U.S.: 3010 Walden Ave., P.O. Box 1325, Buffalo, NY 14269
Canadian: P.O. Box 609, Fort Erie, Ont. L2A 5X3

THE TYCOON
AND THE TOWNIE

Elizabeth Lane

Silhouette
R O M A N C E™
Published by Silhouette Books
America's Publisher of Contemporary Romance

To Millicent, my very first guide to the world of
fairies, mermaids and other marvels.

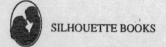 SILHOUETTE BOOKS

ISBN 0-373-19250-9

THE TYCOON AND THE TOWNIE

Copyright © 1997 by Elizabeth Lane

Printed in U.S.A.

Books by Elizabeth Lane

Silhouette Romance

Hometown Wedding #1194
The Tycoon and the Townie #1250

Silhouette Special Edition

Wild Wings, Wild Heart #936

ELIZABETH LANE

has traveled extensively in Latin America, Europe and China, and enjoys bringing these exotic locales to life on the printed page, but she also finds her home state of Utah and other areas of the American West to be fascinating sources for historical romance. Elizabeth loves such diverse activities as hiking and playing the piano, not to mention her latest hobby—belly dancing.

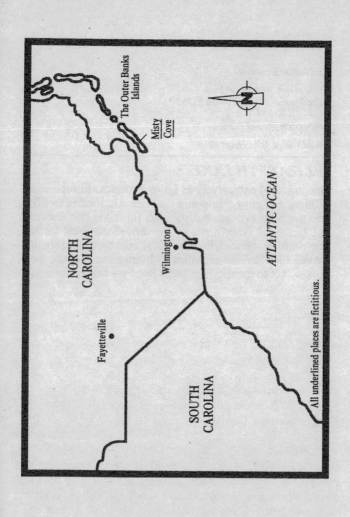

The Outer Banks
Islands

Misty
Cove

ATLANTIC OCEAN

NORTH
CAROLINA

Wilmington

Fayetteville

SOUTH
CAROLINA

All underlined places are fictitious.

Chapter One

"Excuse me, but is my nose on straight?"

The raspy-cello voice was so sensual that for an instant Jefferson Parrish III thought he must still be dreaming. Lulled by cool Atlantic breezes, he had dozed off in one of the big Adirondack chairs on the open verandah, only to be startled awake by this libido-tickling Greta Garbo voice.

A voice that appeared to be coming from a clown.

"What the devil...?" Jeff blinked himself fully awake, expecting the clown to vaporize. No such luck.

"I need to make sure my nose is on straight. I bumped it getting out of the Jeep. Quick—take a look!"

Too startled to argue, Jeff did as he was told. The clown was certainly no Bozo, he observed. Or Ronald McDonald, either. Short and pudgy in a tie-dyed, padded suit and ragged purple wig, she couldn't have stretched over five foot three. White greasepaint and a round, red, rubber nose hid whatever features she might possess—except for her eyes. Surrounded by painted circles, they blazed like oversize twin aquamarines.

Fine and dandy, Jeff groused, easing out of the chair and stretching to his husky six-foot height. But unless some ragtag circus had come to Misty Point, North Carolina, he still had no idea why this dumpy-looking little clown would be standing on his verandah in the middle of an ordinary July afternoon.

"Well?" the hypnotic voice demanded.

Jeff ran an impatient hand through his wiry thatch of prematurely graying hair. "Yes, your nose is on straight. Now, would you mind telling me what the hell you're doing here?"

She appeared startled, though it was hard to tell beneath all that paint. "Uh—you *are* Mr. Jefferson Parrish, aren't you?" she asked.

"Yes," Jeff snapped, none too graciously.

"Then you should be expecting me. My agency sent me. I'm Jo-Jo."

The look he gave her was as blank as his mind.

"The clown you hired for your daughter, Ellen's, birthday party."

"The party—oh, blast..." Jeff remembered dimly that his mother had said something about hiring a party clown, but until this moment, he'd forgotten all about it. That, or he was still asleep, and having this bizarre dream....

"I'm sorry," he muttered. "And yes, you *are* expected."

"Fine. So, where's the party?"

"Around the back, on the lawn. My mother's in charge. She'd be the one who called the agency."

"And how old is little Ellen?" The clown gathered up a lumpy green duffel bag from the front steps and hefted it to her shoulder.

"She's nine."

"Nine!" The phrase she muttered under her breath sounded vaguely like an Irish curse.

"Is anything wrong?"

"It's just that my act usually goes over better with the three- to five-year-old crowd. For nine-year-olds, you should've hired rock musicians!"

"Tell that to my mother. She's in charge. Now, if you'll excuse me..." Jeff stifled a yawn and took a tentative step toward the front door, hoping Yo-Yo, or whatever her name was, would take the hint and head for the party. His blueprints for the new wing of Heath Memorial Hospital were up for review next week. Vacation or no vacation, it was time he went inside and got back to work on them.

He strode across the verandah, struggling to shake off the ennui that had settled over him in this sleepy little seashore town. It had been a mistake, giving in to his mother's suggestion that they summer here, in the old family retreat where he had spent so many boyhood vacations. At first Jeff had nourished the hope that the sea air and familiar surroundings would have a healing effect on them all. But it had been an empty hope. Things had only gotten worse.

Even with the hospital project, there was too little for him to do here. And there were too many memories. Too often lately he'd caught himself pacing the confines of his studio, snarling like a caged bear. The discontent had spread to his daughter, as well. Ellen spent her time roaming the dunes of their private beach like a pale little sea wraith. As for Jeff's mother, she'd thrown herself into projects designed to make their lives seem "all right" again. Projects like this birthday party, for which Ellen had displayed no enthusiasm at all.

Dammit, they should have all stayed home in Raleigh, where they—

"Oh—Mr. Parrish?"

Jeff glanced over his shoulder. The clown was poised on

the verandah's top step, the toes of her enormous, floppy shoes hanging eight inches over the edge.

"One more thing," she said. "Just so you'll be aware. I brought my daughter with me today—not that she'll be a bother to anyone. She's been told to stay in the kitchen with your cook, Floss, until I finish the party show. Floss is a friend of ours, and she said it wasn't a problem. Is that all right with you?"

"It's of no consequence whatsoever. Now, if you'll excuse me, I have a lot of work to do."

For the space of a heartbeat she froze, stung, perhaps, by his brusqueness. Then, determined to be cheerful, she thrust out her cherry red chin. "Work? On such a beautiful day? What a waste of creation! But if that's your choice... Goodbye, Mr. Parrish! The agency will bill you for my time!"

With a toss of her shaggy purple mane, she took one blithe misstep into space, pitched forward and disappeared from sight.

Jeff sprinted to the rail of the verandah to find her sprawled across an azalea bed in a sputtering, tie-dyed heap, her duffel bag lying an arm's length away.

"Are you all right?" he asked, torn between real concern and wondering how much her lawyer would settle for out of court.

"I...think so." She wiggled her hands and feet cautiously, then began to struggle like a high-centered terrapin in a vain effort to get up.

"You're *sure* you're all right?"

"Yes," she muttered, collapsing into the azaleas again. "It's these—idiot shoes! Half the time I can't see where I'm going, and if I fall down, they stick out so far I can't get my knees—under me—"

"And here I thought it was all part of your act!" Jeff

suppressed a bemused smile as he trotted down the steps toward her. "Relax, I'll give you a hand."

"No—don't trouble yourself!" she snapped. "Not when you've got—*so* much work to do. I can get up myself if I take it bit by bit."

"If you insist." Jeff shrugged, then watched with ill-concealed interest as she tumbled onto her side and drew her knees toward her chest. With effort, she managed to roll her big, clown feet under her, push up with her arms and stagger to a standing position.

"There!" she exclaimed, her voice all more intriguing for its breathlessness. "I told you I could do it."

"Independent little twit, aren't you?" Jeff observed dryly as she brushed sprigs of loose grass from her costume.

Her small, ridiculously painted face froze for an instant.

"Independent little twit?" She repeated the words slowly, as if dissecting each syllable. "*Independent little twit?*"

As Jeff watched, the dumpy clown figure seemed to grow visibly taller. Then, suddenly, she spun toward him, her aquamarine eyes flashing cold fire.

"Independent I'll accept as a compliment," she declared icily. "But I'm certainly no twit, Mr. Parrish. I'm a woman alone with a daughter to raise and bills to pay. Jo-Jo the clown helps me pay those bills—but that's something a man like you might not understand. You've probably never had a minute's financial worry in your smug, arrogant, self-satisfied life!"

Before Jeff could gather his wits, she was gone, waddling across the grass like an indignant Jemima Puddleduck in her padded clown suit. He might have laughed—the sight of her was ludicrous enough—but something in her words and her voice had stung him like a smart blow with a riding quirt.

Good Lord, did he really come across as the woman had described him? Smug, arrogant and self-satisfied? Could that be the reason Meredith had—

But never mind, he brought himself up harshly. It was too damned late to do anything about Meredith, and too late to change his own nature. He was what he was, and right now he had work to do. The plans for the new hospital wing lay open on his drafting table, with hours—many, many hours—of changes yet to be done on them.

Closing his mind to the sunlit ocean air, the cry of seabirds and the vanishing figure of the odd little clown, Jeff strode into the house and shut the door firmly behind him.

Summer people!

Kate Valera's thoughts seethed as she shuffled across the broad expanse of lawn. Every year the summer people invaded Misty Point like a flock of chattering, inland birds, flaunting their money and their success as if they owned the town. They opened up the elegant frame homes they called "cottages," raced their Jaguars and Porsches along peaceful back roads and treated the year-rounders like second-rate hired help.

Summer people!

Kate quivered, still feeling the sting of Mr. Jefferson Parrish's high-handed arrogance. She was not sorry she'd put him in his place. For two cents, in fact, she would cheerfully tell the whole pretentious lot of them to—

But what was she thinking? The economic survival of the town depended on these obnoxious visitors. Her own survival depended on them. They bought her beautiful, hand-thrown pots at gallery prices that made the locals gasp. They paid for her performances as Jo-Jo the Clown, with money that one day, she hoped, would finance an education for her daughter, Flannery. Oh, yes, she *needed* these people, and she had precious little choice except to grit her teeth and be nice to them. Saints preserve her!

As she came around the house, Kate spotted the party group seated at tables on the far end of the lawn. Not a very promising bunch, she mused glumly. A dozen bored-looking little girls in sundresses clustered around the soggy remains of cake and ice cream, overseen by a tall, stern-looking woman who seemed to have no idea what to do with them. Jo-Jo would have her work cut out for her today!

They had seen her. Kate waved breezily and broke into her prancing side-to-side clown gait. These kids were about the same age as her daughter, she reminded herself. Maybe she could pretend she was entertaining Flannery, and— But, no, she was deluding herself. These privileged little girls were nothing like Flannery. They had seen everything from first-run Broadway shows to the Ringling Brothers Circus. They would not be impressed by one shabby clown with a bag of simple tricks.

The woman, a stately figure in a lilac afternoon dress, with a visage as humorless as the Statue of Liberty's, left the group and came striding toward her. "You're late!" she snapped, brandishing the antique bull's-eye watch she wore on a gold neck chain. "You were supposed to be here seven minutes ago!"

Sorry! Kate pantomimed, rippling her shoulders and spreading her hands in an elaborate shrug. She wasn't usually silent during her Jo-Jo act, but today it struck her as a useful idea.

"Well, it can't be helped now." The woman's ragged sigh revealed the edge of her own frustration. "Don't just stand there looking silly. You were hired to do a job. Get on with it!''

And with that stirring introduction...

Kate clicked on the portable tape player in her duffel bag, pranced into the open space between the tables and executed a series of spins and fancy heel clicks that would have enthralled any group of three-year-olds. These jaded little dollies didn't even blink. Well, maybe the juggling act would impress them; though, in truth, she had her doubts.

Scooping a net of multicolored balls out of the duffel, Kate lined them up on the grass in front of her. For a furtive moment her eyes scanned the young audience. It was easy enough to single out Ellen, the birthday girl. She was seated at the center table wearing a gold paper crown and a wretched expression. She was a beautiful child, Kate observed, with a pale oval face, long black hair and her father's unsettling gray eyes.

*Unsettling...*now, where had *that* come from?

Forcing herself to concentrate, Kate went through the elaborate motions of counting the balls. *One, two, three, four, five.* She paused and shook her head in a show of bewilderment. *One, two, three, four, five.* She matched the count on her fingers, her actions indicating clearly that one ball was missing.

Aha! I know where it is! With a crafty expression on her painted face, she crept toward Ellen Parrish. The girl's lips parted uncertainly as Kate's gloved hand reached beneath the straight, dark silk of her hair and, with a triumphant flourish, produced the sixth ball.

A wave of giggles, underscored by none-too-kindly whispers, rippled around the tables. Too late, Kate glimpsed Ellen's unshed tears and realized what she had done. She had embarrassed the sensitive child in front of these clannish girls who were not even pretending to be her friends.

Heartsick, Kate battled the urge to gather the sad little creature in her arms and beg her forgiveness. There was no way to undo what she had already done. But at least she could make sure the other girls got equal treatment. Oh, yes, she could, and she would.

Armed with a new sense of purpose, Kate realigned the colored balls on the grass, scooped up the first three and launched into her juggling routine. That little Shirley Temple blonde in the pink pinafore, the one who was smirking like a fox in a hen yard—yes, she would be next.

Warm and restless in his upstairs studio, Jeff Parrish swung away from his drafting table and wandered to the window. Cracking it open, though not so far that the breeze would scatter his papers, he filled his senses with the clean, salty smell of the ocean.

He had loved that scent as a boy—loved it so much that he'd dreamed of running off to a life of exploration and piracy on the high seas. It had never happened, of course. Boys grew up to be practical men. Dreams changed, or they died. Now the smell of the sea only reminded Jeff of how far he had journeyed from his boyhood, how mechanical his life had become, and how empty.

The window gave him a bird's-eye view of Ellen's birthday celebration on the lawn below. Judging from the looks of things, it wasn't going particularly well. His mother had planned the party with the idea of finding Ellen some "proper" friends. She had invited girls from Misty Point's most prominent summer families. As always, the dear woman had meant well, but there was one reality she had failed to grasp. Most of the young guests knew each other from summers that spanned as far back as they could remember. Sweet, shy Ellen was a newcomer, a stranger to them all.

When Jeff's daughter had declared she did not want a birthday party, he had dismissed her attitude as plain stubbornness. Only now, looking down at the group on the lawn, did he truly understand her reasons. His Ellen sat alone, isolated in the seat of honor, while the other guests formed their own clusters on either side of her. None of the girls seemed to be paying her any attention at all.

Jeff ached with helpless worry. A more outgoing child might have bridged the gap and made friends. But Ellen had experienced so much aloneness in her young life that she only invited more. Worse, there seemed to be nothing he could do for her. The therapist said these things took time. But how much time? It had been more than eighteen months since Meredith—

Brooding over the past wouldn't help, he reminded himself harshly. Ellen could only heal in her own time. As for him, the single antidote to what had happened was work.

As he turned to leave the window, his attention was drawn once more to the clown. She was prancing before the group, juggling a rainbow of multicolored balls. Jo-Jo, or whoever she was, had been right about nine-year-olds, he conceded. The lady had drawn one tough audience. But at least she was in there pitching. Not only was her juggling ability impressive, but she was making a real effort to involve the girls.

He watched as one of the balls disappeared into thin air, only to be plucked magically from behind one little blonde's ear. The young audience giggled—more at the girl, Jeff suspected, than at the trick itself, but at least they were laughing. Jo-Jo the Clown knew her stuff.

Giving in to an impulse, he settled himself against the window to watch. A vague, yearning tingle passed through him as he remembered the husky timbre of her voice and the flash of those intriguing eyes. It would be an interesting challenge to find out what she looked like under that ridiculous wig and makeup. She *sounded* like a cuddly Lauren Bacall—but then, a man's imagination played strange tricks. He was probably just as well off not knowing.

She had finished the juggling routine and was digging something else out of her lumpy green duffel. From where he stood, it appeared to be a box of long, thin balloons. Yes—she was blowing them up now, twisting them into clever animal shapes for each of the girls. As entertainment, it was corny, but her skill was mesmerizing. Although he would never have believed it possible, she had those jaded youngsters in the palms of her deft little hands. She damned near had *him!*

For another minute, perhaps, he remained glued to the window, fascinated by the puzzle of the woman beneath Jo-Jo the Clown. There was something about the quaint little figure—an air of grace and spirit....

But enough of this time wasting; he had work to do!

Reluctantly Jeff forced himself away from the view and back to his drafting table. Shutting out the distractions of the warm summer day and the disturbing little clown, he refocused his thoughts on the hospital plans. The ideas were just beginning to flow again when he heard his mother's no-nonsense tread coming up the stairs.

"Jeff!—" Her agitated breathing told him she was upset. "You've got to come down and help me! It's Ellen! She's left her own party! She's gone!"

Now what?

Kate rummaged in her duffel bag, wondering how much longer she could hold this show together on her own, with no guest of honor and no hostess.

She had glanced up from inflating the last few balloons to see Ellen Parrish slip away from her table and wander off in the direction of the house. If the other girls had noticed, none of them had spoken up, and Kate wasn't about to call attention to the poor child, who was more than likely just feeling sick to her stomach. It was only a few minutes later, when Ellen's grandmother caught sight of the empty chair, that the strain had burst into the open.

"Where *could* that child have gone?" she'd exclaimed, visibly at her wit's end. "You—Clown—carry on while I go and find out what's gotten into her!"

Jo-Jo hadn't been doing too badly up to that point, but now things were beginning to come apart. The girls were whispering and giggling like a flock of restless budgie birds, and Kate knew the cheap pocket toys she'd brought along as favors would be no help at all. Groping in the duffel bag, her hand closed on the spare makeup case she carried for touch-ups. Suddenly she had an idea.

"Say, who wants to be a clown?" she exclaimed, speaking for the first time as she opened the case on a tabletop. "Come on, I need a volunteer!"

The girls buzzed and twittered, then shoved one of their peers to the center of the circle. It was the little Shirley Temple blonde Kate had noticed earlier.

"So, what's your name, dear?" she asked in an encouraging tone.

"Muffet. Muffet Bodell. My father is—"

"How would you like to be a clown, Muffet?"

"Uh, I guess it would be—"

"Wonderful!" Kate plopped the little girl onto a chair and swiftly fashioned a makeshift cape out of a tablecloth. "Come closer and watch, girls. Then we'll see who'd like to be next! Now...the first step in putting on clown makeup is to rub on lots and lots of white..."

The other girls crowded around, fascinated, as their playmate acquired a clown-white face, red cheeks and big, round, painted eyes. Kate was just adding some eyelashes when she heard a horrified gasp from behind her.

"No! Oh, no, no, no!"

She turned around to see Mrs. Parrish descending on her like a lavender steam locomotive. "How could you do this?" she snapped. "Muffet is Congressman Bodell's daughter. Her mother is coming by to pick her up and take her to a wedding. She'll be here any minute—and just *look* at the child!"

Kate grabbed a jar of cold cream and a handful of tissues. "I'm sorry, but no one told me a thing. We were just—"

"Here, I'll do that!" The woman snatched the tissues out of Kate's hand. "You're already in enough trouble! I just talked to the cook. Ellen has disappeared with *your* daughter!"

"Flannery?" Kate's heart plummeted. "But I told her to stay right there with Floss! She wouldn't just disobey me and—"

"Well, it seems she did! Floss told me that Ellen wandered into the kitchen and the two of them started talking. The next time Floss turned around, they were both gone! My son's out looking for them now, but I'm warning you, if anything's happened to my granddaughter, I'll hold you responsible!"

Worry, chagrin and indignation yanked at Kate's emotions. "Look, I know you're upset, but they shouldn't be in any danger. Flannery knows the neighborhood and the beaches. She may have disobeyed me, but she's not foolhardy enough to—"

"Never mind!" the woman snapped. "The party is over! I'll look after these girls until their parents come for them.

Meanwhile, if you have any notion where your daughter might have taken Ellen—''

Kate's frayed emotions snapped. "Merciful heaven, you're making it sound as if Flannery's kidnapped her!" she burst out against her better judgment. "If you think you can just stand there and imply that—''

"I'm implying nothing! I just want my granddaughter found forthwith! Now if you wouldn't mind—''

"I'm going. And don't worry, I'll find them." Kate waddled off toward the house, clutching the shattered remains of her dignity. She could feel the eyes of the little girls drilling into her back like bullets from a firing squad. For all she knew, they'd concluded she was part of some evil conspiracy to lure small children with her clown act, then spirit them away into slavery or worse. If such a story got around, Jo-Jo would be finished for the season, maybe for good.

That Flannery!

What could have gotten into the child? Kate brooded as she trudged around to the kitchen entrance, intending to speak with Floss. Flannery was usually so obedient. Why on earth would she—

Oof!

The collision with Jeff Parrish was a solid blow, as if she'd run headlong into a brick wall. Kate reeled backward, the physical shock triggering an unexpected rush of tears. After this ghastly afternoon, all she wanted was to find Flannery, pile the clown things into the Jeep, and drive home. The last thing she needed was another encounter with this irritating man!

"Would you like to try that maneuver again? I don't think I've quite gotten the hang of it." He was standing on the kitchen stoop, making no move to let her pass.

Kate's defiant gaze measured his muscular frame, mov-

ing upward to a square, suntanned face with a nose that
would have looked more at home on a prizefighter than the
architect she'd been told he was. It was not a glamorous
face, not even a handsome face in the usual sense—but he
did have unsettling gray eyes. A closer look confirmed that
they were the same color as his daughter's—except that
Ellen's eyes were like stormy sea clouds. Jeff Parrish's eyes
were the cold steel gray of bridge girders.

Kate realized she was staring at him. She groped for a
clever remark and came up empty except for the emotions
that threatened to bubble over and disgrace her on the spot.

"Oh, get out of my way!" she muttered, starting to edge
around him. "I haven't got time for this!"

Only then did she notice his shirt—a soft polo, obviously
expensive, its color an immaculate ice blue against his
golden skin—

Immaculate, except for the big, ugly makeup smear in
front, where her face had slammed into his chest.

"Oh!" She noticed it the same time he did. "I'm sorry—
no, sorry doesn't say it! I'm mortified! I'll pay to have it
cleaned—"

"Cleaned?" He craned his neck, examining the spot.
"No, wait! This could have possibilities! Maybe we could
add a stencil saying 'I Bumped Into Jo-Jo the Clown.' You
know, sort of like those old Tammi Faye shirts that were
hot sellers a few years back. Think what great publicity it
would be for you, Jo-Jo."

"My name isn't Jo-Jo." Kate popped off the rubber nose
and jammed it irritably into her pocket. "It's Kathryn. Kate.
Kate Valera."

"I Bumped Into Kate Valera. No, I'm sorry. It doesn't
have quite the same ring to it."

"Are you always this sarcastic?"

"Only when it suits me." The barest hint of a spark

flashed in his eyes, only to vanish when he spoke again. "If you're looking for your daughter, she's not in the kitchen."

"I know. Your mother seems to think that Flannery has spirited your Ellen away and is holding her for ransom in some murky cave! I came by the house to see what I could learn from Floss. Then I'm going to look for the girls. So if you've still got work to do—"

"I've already spoken with Floss. From what she told me, I'd say our two young fugitives have gone to the beach. I was just on my way to look for them. If that chip on your shoulder isn't weighing you down too much, you're welcome to come with me."

Kate's jaw dropped. "Chip on *my* shoulder..." she sputtered. "Of all the—"

"That's what I said." He steered her away from the house with a firm grip on her upper arm. "Now, stop arguing and come along. We've got a couple of lost daughters to find!"

Chapter Two

"So how long have you been, uh, clowning around?" Jeff realized the question was inane as soon as he'd asked it. First sarcasm, now lame wordplays. Thank goodness he wasn't trying to impress this lady.

"Doing Jo-Jo, you mean?" She had a cute nose without that silly rubber ball. Small and pert—and was that a tiny freckle on the end, where the paint had rubbed off? He found himself itching for a closer look.

"Uh-huh. I saw your juggling act from the window. Pretty impressive."

"My grandfather taught me how to juggle when I was ten." She marched along beside him, picking up each clumsy shoe and putting it down flat to keep from stumbling in the long sea grass. "As for the rest of the act, about five years ago, I sent off for a video course in clowning. After a few months' practice, I made the costume, bought the wig and makeup, and *voilà!* Jo-Jo was born!"

She paused to work her way around a thick clump of sedge. Jeff slowed his pace to wait for her, savoring the uneasy truce that had settled between them. Whatever she might look like under that clown getup, she struck him as a plucky little woman, smart and down to earth. And sexy, he conceded—which was damned strange, considering he'd never seen her face, let alone her figure.

"Jo-Jo's been a good sideline," she continued, "at least in the summer. If you count church fund-raisers and passing out cheese dip samples at Piggly Wiggly, I do two or three appearances a week. But I lied to you about one thing earlier this afternoon."

"About my being smug, arrogant and self-satisfied?"

"Hardly." Her eyes flashed danger.

Jeff faked an indifferent shrug. "All right. I'm waiting to hear your confession."

"I lied about the money I earn as Jo-Jo. It doesn't go to pay bills. I put every cent of it into my daughter's college fund."

"And you lied about that—for shame! What could have possessed you?" He studied the stubborn outline of her profile, thinking it was extraordinary of her, going through this idiot clown charade for her child's future. He would have liked to tell her so, but something held him back. This woman was proud, he sensed—too proud to welcome such a compliment.

"It just came out," she said. "But I don't like lying. Not even to you."

"Oh, thanks a lot." Jeff struck up the side of the first dune, feeling the sea wind like the stroke of cool fingers in his hair. From beyond the crest, he could hear the roll and hiss of the incoming tide. Silently he prayed that two venturesome little girls would have the sense to stay back from the waves.

"What do you do the rest of the year?" he asked, shifting the conversation back to neutral ground.

"The rest of the year, I batten down my house against the nor'easters and mostly hole up in my pottery studio," she answered. "What gave you the idea the girls went to the beach? Was it something Floss told you?"

"Right—careful!" Jeff grabbed her elbow to steady her on the sandy slope. Her arm felt lean and strong. He liked touching her. "It struck me as a bit strange," he said, "but Floss claimed she overheard them talking about...mermaids."

"Mermaids!" Her laugh was low and cool, with a delicious little bite to it, like iced Kahlúa on a sweltering summer day. "I should have guessed! My daughter loves mermaids! She's writing a book about them!"

"A book?" Jeff felt a hillock of sand give way beneath his step, filling his shoe with grit. He cursed mildly under his breath. "I thought we were looking for a youngster."

"We are." The glance she flashed him was ripe with mystery. Then she, too, stumbled in the cascade of loose sand. Her big, clown feet splayed in opposite directions, and she went down hard on her padded rump.

Caught between gallantry and amusement, Jeff stretched out a hand. She reached up tentatively, then withdrew, shaking her shaggy, purple mane. "It's no use! I can't climb sand dunes in these idiot shoes. I'll have to get rid of them and catch up with you—go on."

"Go on? And leave a lady in distress? I'd never live it down. Here..." Jeff slid to the sand at her feet and began tugging at her tightly knotted shoelaces. She sank back against the dune in tacit consent, resting, but far from relaxed.

"Are you sure you should be out here alone with me?" she ventured. "Your mother was upset enough when our daughters disappeared together. If her son vanishes, too..."

She broke off, her small, even teeth pressing her lower lip as if she'd said too much.

"I'm a big boy. Even my mother knows that." Jeff tugged off one of the platter-sized shoes and the thick cotton sweat sock she wore underneath. Her narrow-boned foot was as pink and innocent as a child's. For a heartbeat, he cradled it like a captive seabird in his big, brown hand, feeling the warmth of her skin against his palm. A subtle electric pulse trickled up his arm, awakening his whole body to a quivering awareness of—

No, this was *not* a good idea.

"I realize she comes on a little stridently," he said, reaching for the other shoe, "but don't misjudge my mother. She never expected to be raising another child at the age of sixty. She does her best, and I know how much she cares for Ellen, but I daresay it hasn't been an easy adjustment for either of them. Sometimes that shows."

Her blue-green eyes studied him from their painted circles, their expression as unreadable as a cat's. Seconds ticked by before she spoke.

"Do you mind my asking what happened to Ellen's mother?"

"She died over a year ago—in an automobile accident." Jeff tugged at the stubbornly knotted shoelace. No use going into the ugly details—Meredith's drinking, her affair with one of his clients, the bitter divorce that would have become final six days after she crashed her Mercedes into an oncoming truck....

"I'm sorry," said the clown.

"We—were all sorry." Jeff jerked the knot loose and twisted off the other shoe. The sock came with it. "Come on," he muttered. "We'd better get moving if we want to find our daughters."

He gave her a hand up, surprised at the power in her thin

fingers. Then he waited while she knotted the ends of her shoelaces and flung the shoes over her shoulder. Her bare feet gripped the sand as they mounted the dune.

Kathryn. Kate. Kate Valera. The name had a nice ring to it. Almost as nice as her voice. And her eyes.

But what was he thinking? He wasn't ready for another woman in his life, let alone a free-spirited throwback to the seventies, who made pottery, masqueraded as a clown and, for all he knew, could look like a basset hound under that greasepaint.

Oh, sooner or later he planned to remarry—to provide a mother for Ellen, if nothing else. But the few dates he'd tried in recent months had been disasters, underscoring the fact that he was still too raw, too angry for a new relationship.

But why was he being so damned analytical? He had no intention of dating this woman. He was making polite conversation with her, that was all. They would find their little girls, go their separate ways, and if he passed her on the street later, without that crazy clown paint, the odds were he would not even recognize her.

"What about you?" he asked. "You said you were alone."

"Flannery's father—he, uh, we separated before she was born."

"Flannery?" he asked, bringing her back. "As in Flannery O'Connor?"

"Uh-huh. She's my favorite author. Have you read her?"

"My freshman English professor assigned us a couple of her stories." Jeff could not remember the titles or what the stories had been about. Now he found himself wishing he'd paid them more attention.

"So your Flannery's an author, too."

"Absolutely. She's already filled up four spiral notebooks. Who knows? We may have a bestseller on our hands, in which case, Jo-Jo can retire, and Flannery can put *me* through college!''

''But mermaids! Lord, why doesn't she write about something sensible, or at least real?''

Blue lightning sparked in her eyes. ''Watch it, mister! Flannery happens to be the world's foremost authority on mermaids!''

''Then I can't imagine that she and Ellen would have much in common. Ellen has been raised the way my parents raised me—in the world of truth and reality. No talking teapots. No animals with human personalities. No dragons, no fairy princesses—''

''And only anatomically correct teddy bears, I suppose! Good grief, that poor child—''

''Excuse me.'' Jeff had gone rigid. ''Are you presuming to tell me how to raise my daughter?''

She turned on him at the top of the dune, the sea wind ruffling her wild, purple hair. ''I'm not presuming to tell you anything, you stuffy, pompous—''

''*You* watch it, lady!''

She faced him almost toe-to-toe, undaunted by his size and his anger. ''You wouldn't listen if I *did* tell you! But then, why should I have to tell you anything? Just look at your little girl! Look how unhappy she is—''

''And you're suggesting that a dose of fantasy will cure that?'' He thrust his own steel into her intense blue-green gaze. ''Answer me this, then, Kate Valera, or Jo-Jo the Clown, or whoever you think you are! Will fantasy bring back Ellen's mother? Will fantasy give her a real family again?''

Her eyes held steady, but her lips had begun to tremble in the center of her painted clown smile. ''I don't know how to answer that," she whispered, "except to say that I—I feel sorry for you!"

She spun away from him and stalked off along the crest of the dune. Jeff glared after the slight, lumpy figure, his mind still hearing the little catch in her voice. If it had been tears, then the woman was an emotional fool, he told himself. The last thing he and Ellen needed was pity, especially from someone who knew so little about her.

Mermaids indeed! No, Ellen didn't need that kind of nonsense either! According to the therapist, what she needed was to *accept* the reality of her mother's loss, not escape from it. If he could just make that mule-headed little clown person understand—

"Wait up!" he called after her. "You're not getting away without hearing my side of—"

"I see our daughters," she said quietly, glancing back over her shoulder as if she hadn't heard him. "They're out on the end of the spit. Look…"

Jeff's gaze followed the direction of her pointing arm, anxiously scanning the long, pale crescent of beach below the dunes. About two hundred yards away, on a rocky spit of land that jutted into the pounding surf, he saw them—two dark specks, perched on the flat top of a high rock, oblivious to the waves that crashed around them.

"Damn!" Jeff's fear exploded as anger through his clenched teeth. "Look at that tide! Don't they realize it'll be over the spit in a minute or two? They'll be cut off from the beach! And if they try to get back then—" He cupped his hands to his mouth, and was about to shout when he felt her cool, taut fingers on his bare arm.

"They won't be able to hear you over the surf," she said. "Come on, we've got to get down there!"

Without waiting for him to follow, she bounded down the slope of the dune, half-sliding, half-falling in her tie-dyed clown suit. Jeff charged after her, each step setting off a small avalanche of sand. He knew this beach well. The girls were safe enough on their high rock, but if they realized their predicament and tried to cross the wave-swept spit, they could be washed into the ocean.

Kate had reached the level beach and was running full-out, her bare feet spattering the edge of the tide foam. Jeff could see the girls clearly now—Ellen, with her dark hair and pale yellow dress; carrot-topped Flannery, wearing shorts and a green T-shirt. They were sitting close together, staring out to sea, oblivious to the danger behind them.

Sheets of water were already whipping over the spit. He didn't dare shout now or do anything that might draw the girls' attention. If they saw him and tried to come back on their own, the waves would sweep them away.

Kate was flagging. Jeff saw her stumble, then catch herself and plunge ahead. With a surge of effort, he sprinted past her and raced toward the spit, silently praying the girls would stay put until he could reach them.

Gritty seawater swirled around his ankles as he pounded into the surf. The tide was coming in fast now. Its powerful undertow sucked at Jeff's legs as he waded deeper. Out of the corner of his eye he glimpsed Kate. She had plunged recklessly into the waves and was struggling after him. With a scowl, he motioned her back. The water was getting deep. It would be rough going for her in that soggy clown getup, and the last thing he needed was another body to rescue and haul ashore.

The girls had spotted him. Ellen was waving, dancing up and down like an excited jack-in-the-box. Flannery, he noticed, was hanging back with more caution. One hand gripped the skirt of Ellen's sundress, as if to prevent her from leaping into the sea. The other hand clutched a brown spiral notebook.

"Stay put!" Jeff shouted, but his words were sucked into the roar of exploding surf. Sand dissolved under his feet as he rounded the narrow curve of the spit. The water hissed and clawed at his legs like a demented wildcat.

An eternity seemed to pass before he reached the rock. Looking up, he could see Ellen. She was straining toward him, her gray eyes round with fear. Only Flannery's terrier grip on her skirt kept her from losing her balance and toppling into the waves.

"Come on!" Jeff held out his arms, and Ellen clambered into them, clinging to his neck like a frightened monkey. Shifting her to a piggyback position, he reached upward for Flannery.

Kate's daughter hesitated. Her right hand clutched the notebook as her narrow, hazel eyes measured the distance between them. Then, with the fearlessness of an acrobat, she flung herself into space.

Jeff tensed as he caught her against his chest. She was taller than Ellen and lighter, her body all bone and sinew in his arms. Her freckled features were as sharp as an elf's below the kinky bonfire of her hair. Even now, Jeff could not help wondering how much this rather strange child resembled her mother.

Water churned around his hips, threatening to drag him down with his precious burden. "Hang on," he muttered, battling for a foothold on the treacherous bottom. "Whatever happens, don't let go of me!" He staggered toward the beach, each step an adventure in peril. The girls weren't heavy, but their weight was enough to throw him off balance. One false step, and they would all go down.

Through a curtain of sea spray, he could see Kate. She had left the beach and was toiling toward him through the battering surf. He wanted to shout at her, to warn her to stay back, but Kate Valera was a stubborn woman, and he was carrying her daughter. Even if she could hear him, Jeff knew she wouldn't listen.

The water grew shallower, but no less violent, as the slope of the beach rose under his feet. Kate had almost reached him. She was stretching out her arms to take Flannery when a wave struck her from the side, knocking her off her feet and flinging her toward him.

Jeff had no free hand to grab her. He fought for balance as she crashed into him and went down. "Hang on to me!" he shouted over the roar of the surf. Her arms clutched his legs as he staggered out of the water, dragging her with him.

It took a moment for Jeff to realize they were safe, all of them, on the warm, dry sand. Still clutching her notebook, Flannery let go of Jeff's neck and dropped lightly to her feet. Ellen clung, trembling, to his back. He unpeeled her arms and eased her downward.

Kate sprawled on the sand. Her wig was askew, her makeup smeared. The padding under her clown suit drooped with seawater. She looked so pathetic, and so ludicrous, that Jeff might have laughed—except there was nothing funny about the situation.

"Flannery Valera, you come here this minute!" She pushed herself to a sitting position, eyes sparking like flints. Her orange-haired daughter shuffled forward, eyes downcast, notebook clutched to her chest.

"What do you think you were doing, young lady?" Kate demanded. "You were told to stay in the kitchen! When we get home, you and I are going to have a long—"

"Oh, please don't punish Flannery!" Ellen darted between them like a fragile, yellow butterfly. "It was my fault! I asked her to take me out on the rocks! She said no at first, but I begged her—"

"Why?" Jeff placed a hand on his child's shoulder and

turned her around to face him. "Why on earth would you want to go out on those dangerous rocks, Ellen?"

Ellen's velvet eyes held an expression Jeff had never seen before—a look of pure, radiant wonder.

"Flannery told me about the mermaids. She said that if you sit on the rocks and listen with all your heart, sometimes you can hear them singing—"

"Ellen!" Jeff groaned in dismay. "That's nonsense, and you know it! There's no such thing as—"

"But you're wrong, Daddy!" Ellen's small frame quivered with certainty. "They're real! I heard them out there! I listened with all my heart, and I heard the mermaids singing!"

Kate trudged miserably up the side of the dune. Her sand-caked costume hung like a sack of potatoes on her sweltering body. The saltwater residue on her skin was beginning to itch, and her damp wig had been discovered by a colony of friendly sand flies. All she wanted to do, at this point, was find the Jeep, go home, take a long, cool shower—and nail her daughter's little freckled hide to the living room wall.

The afternoon had been a string of disasters, but this was the capper. For the most part, she enjoyed Flannery's creative nature and allowed her youthful imagination free rein. But when Flannery's imagination overruled good judgment and put her and another child in danger—

"Are you going to make it all right?" Jeff Parrish glanced over his shoulder with a superior scowl—his usual expression, Kate surmised. To avoid his gaze, she had deliberately dropped behind him in their trek up the dune. Her position, however, gave her a mouth-watering view of his rugged shoulders, tapering back and taut, muscular buttocks. Jefferson Parrish III might be a pain in the fanny, but he was also, Kate conceded, a world-class hunk.

"Kate?" He was waiting for an answer to his question.

"I'll be—fine," Kate muttered, blowing a sand fly out of her face. "Just get me back to my Jeep so I can drive home and forget this whole wretched afternoon!"

"You didn't have to go into the water," he said. "With the heavy surf, and you in all that padding, you should have known what would happen."

"I wasn't thinking about myself," Kate snapped. "I was concerned about my daughter—and yours. And speaking of our daughters, how far ahead of us are they? Can you see them?"

"They're just over the top of the dune. They'll be fine."

"Except that Flannery is probably filling your Ellen's head with more of that fantasy nonsense—oh, I saw your face when Ellen said she'd heard the mermaids. Your expression was definitely not a pretty sight."

"Here." He reached back, caught her hand, and yanked her up to his own level on the dune. "I want to be able to talk to you without getting a kink in my neck," he explained.

"So talk." Kate feigned an indifferent shrug, her salt-soaked bra straps chafing her tender flesh. "See if you can tell me anything I haven't already figured out."

"I was hoping that chip on your shoulder had washed off in the ocean."

"No such luck. But at least I'm willing to listen."

"I'll take that into account." He climbed in silence for the next few steps, his fingers still gripping hers. His palm was as smooth as fine Italian leather—but then, Jefferson Parrish III had probably never lifted anything heavier than a cricket bat. Maybe that was how he'd broken that quirkily gorgeous nose of his.

"This probably sounds stuffy, but I don't know how else to explain it," he said, his free hand swinging her clown shoes, which he'd gallantly fished out of the surf. "We Parrishes are raised with certain values—ethics, if you will. We take pride in passing those values down from one generation to the next."

Like congenital arrogance, Kate almost said, but she managed to bite back the words.

"Oh, I know what you're thinking. But family tradition is a serious matter. I was raised the way my father was raised, and his father and grandfather before him—to value honesty and hard work, to do one's best in every effort and to shun anything that smacks of falsehood or frivolity—"

"Such as fairy tales. And mermaids."

"Exactly." He sounded so smug that Kate could have punched him.

"But Ellen's just a little girl—"

"We raise our girls the same way. My older sister is a neurosurgeon. One of my aunts was a civil engineer. Another taught physics at Radcliffe—"

"And what if Ellen doesn't want to become a surgeon or an engineer or a physicist?"

His penetrating scowl knotted the thick, dark brows above his steely eyes. "You're missing the point, Kate. Ellen will be free to become whatever she chooses. But as her father, it's my duty to see that her choices are based on sound, realistic principles."

"I see." Kate wiped a sweat bead off her nose. Overhead a pair of gulls wheeled and cried in a giddy mating dance. "And what if Ellen makes mistakes?" she asked. "What then?"

"If I do my job as a parent, that's unlikely to happen. Most mistakes, after all, are based on unrealistic expectations."

"But hasn't anyone in your family ever made a mistake? For heaven's sake, haven't *you* ever made a mistake?"

She felt his hand go rigid, then withdraw from hers as they rounded the top of the dune. "You ask too many questions, Kate Valera," he said coldly. "Come on, let's catch up with our daughters and get you back to your Jeep."

Kate clung to her silence, keeping a tight rein on her emotions as they trooped down the leeward slope toward the house. Jeff Parrish was the last person who deserved her sympathy, she told herself. The man was too cocksure, too boastful of a family tradition that turned children into little automatons with no freedom to dream and imagine. Worse, he was raising his sensitive daughter to be a copy of his cold, success-driven self. The whole situation was deplorable!

So why, as her gaze outlined the back of his elegantly rugged head, was her mind flitting through visions of cradling that head in the warm furrow between her breasts while her fingers tunneled the rich, dark silver of his hair?...

Merciful heaven, maybe *she* was the one who needed a healthy dose of reality!

She could see the girls now. They were skipping down the slope of the dune, hand in hand, as if they'd been friends for years. And even that was odd, Kate reflected. Flannery had always been a loner, choosing the world of her own creative imagination over the company of other children. What would draw her to a shy child like Ellen Parrish?

But the answer made no difference, Kate reminded herself bitterly. After today's fiasco, the two little girls would not be allowed to see each other again.

Mrs. Parrish had come out of the house. She strode across the lawn like a clipper under full sail, her purple dress fluttering in the afternoon breeze. Where the grass lost itself at the foot of the dune, she paused, wringing her hands in a classic portrait of agitation.

"Ellen!" she called. "Where have you been, child? Don't you realize what bad manners it shows, wandering away from your little guests like that? If you want those nice young ladies to be your friends—"

"It's all right, Mother." Jeff had sprinted ahead to catch up with the girls, leaving Kate to trail in at her own pace. "I'll speak with Ellen alone after she's had a chance to think about what she did." He turned on his daughter with an imperious frown. "Upstairs with you now, Ellen. You're not to come down again until we've talked. Understand?"

"Can't Flannery come with me?" Ellen clung to her new friend's hand, eyes wide and imploring.

"I'm sorry, Ellen, but Flannery has to go home now." Kate elected to play the meanie—anything to end this miserable farce and make her getaway.

"But she can come back tomorrow, can't she?" Ellen persisted. "Oh, please let her come!"

"Go upstairs, Ellen." Jeff's eyes were granite slits. *"Now."*

With a heartrending sob, Ellen broke her grip on Flannery's hand and fled toward the house.

"Mom, can't I—"

"Be still, Flannery, you've caused enough trouble for one afternoon." Kate clasped her daughter's shoulder. Then, struggling for dignity in her smeared makeup and waterlogged costume, she squared her chin and turned back toward Jefferson Parrish III and his imposing mother.

"We'll be going now," she declared. "And please don't worry about paying the agency for my time, Mrs. Parrish. I'll make sure they know that this performance was on...me."

It was all Kate could do to get the words out before the waves of anger and humiliation swept over her. Jeff Parrish held out her shoes. She snatched them out of his hand and spun away, her throat jerking as she led her daughter across the lawn to the road, where the Jeep was parked.

Summer people!

Chapter Three

Jeff was hauling chairs and tables into the storage shed when he stumbled over the green duffel lying open on the grass. Only after he'd caught his balance did he realize what he'd found. "Damn," he muttered, his emotions slamming between dismay and a strange, primitive elation. "Damn."

He stood still for a moment, the lonesome cry of a kittiwake echoing in his ears. Inky clouds were swirling in over the dunes. The breeze carried the cool smell of rain. Kate would need the duffel before her next Jo-Jo performance, he reminded himself. He would have to get it back to her.

Jeff exhaled slowly, then, drawn by an urge too strong to resist, lowered himself to a crouch and began rummaging through the contents of the faded canvas bag. If he could find an address, or a phone number—

But who was he kidding? It was plain male curiosity that was driving this search. The odd little clown with the sexy voice had gotten to him in a most unsettling way, and he was looking for a clue—any clue—about the woman beneath that padding and greasepaint. A driver's license photo, an article of clothing...

But the bag held no surprises. There was nothing inside except clown props—a small boom box and an assortment of tapes, the fluorescent balls from the juggling act, a sack of leftover balloons, a bag of cheap party favors and a battered tin fishing-tackle box that contained brushes, tissues, cold cream and tubes of greasy stage makeup. There was nothing of real interest—except for a name and address scratched inside the tackle box lid.

Frank Valera, 81 Seacove Road, Misty Point, N.C.

Jeff frowned pensively as he latched the box and zipped it inside the duffel bag. Kate had mentioned that she was single. So who was Frank Valera? Her brother? Her ex?

But what did that matter? Jeff reminded himself as he tossed the duffel in the trunk of his silver-gray BMW and slammed the lid. Kate's private life was none of his business. He would return her things, drive home, and that would be the end of it.

The end?

The end of *what?*

For Pete's sake, he barely knew Kate Valera. He wasn't even sure what she looked like. He was making altogether too much of this, Jeff berated himself as he carted the last few folding chairs into the shed and padlocked the door. Maybe he'd spent too many months living like a blasted monk, cloistered in his work. Maybe it was time he came out of his shell and found himself a woman—a genteel, socially accomplished lady who would set a fine example for his daughter.

The wind was picking up. It raked Jeff's hair as he strode toward the house. It rippled the grass and lashed his face with the first cool raindrops. Lightning crackled blue fire above the dunes, its resounding thunderclap echoing over the ghostly hiss of the ocean.

Mermaids!

Yes, it was time he had that talk with Ellen.

The rain was splattering down by the time Jeff reached the front steps. He sprinted across the wet verandah and hurried inside through the front door.

The house was silent except for the staccato patter of raindrops against the glass. Jeff was shutting an open window when he remembered that his mother had gone out for early dinner and a movie with Mrs. Frances Appleton, who lived up the road. Floss, the cook, had the evening off—so much the better, Jeff resolved. He would build a fire, then make Ellen some hot cocoa and toasted cheese sandwiches. The two of them could enjoy an evening alone reading or playing a few games of checkers, and there would be plenty of opportunity to talk her out of this mermaid nonsense before bedtime.

There was the matter of Kate Valera's bag. But—yes—he could return it after his mother came home. Maybe he would give Kate a call about it later if her number was in the book. The thought of hearing that delicious, raspy little voice in his ear...

"Ellen..." he shouted from the foot of the staircase. "Hey, come on down, and I'll make us some supper!"

The only answer was the sound of rain.

"Ellen?" He started up the stairs, wondering why she hadn't replied. He'd been a bit harsh with her earlier, but it wasn't like his daughter to sulk.

"Hey, answer me! This isn't funny!" He reached the landing and paused, listening. Outside, thunder boomed across the sky and raindrops splattered the wooden shingles. Inside, the silence was louder than the storm.

"Ellen!" He raced down the hall toward the closed door

of her room. Maybe she'd fallen asleep and couldn't hear him. Maybe...

His heart stopped as he reached the door and flung it open. Ellen's small neat room, with its white ruffled bedspread and framed Renoir prints, was empty.

Kate stepped out of the shower, flung a towel around her short, auburn hair and shrugged into her thick, green terry robe. The steamy air surrounded her like a blanket. She inhaled its damp warmth, forcing the afternoon's events to the back of her mind. Yes, she was doing better. Maybe after a cup of good, hot herbal tea, she would feel almost human again.

She opened the bathroom window to clear the steam. Outside, the storm had grown savage. Rain battered the sides of the small clapboard house. Wind lashed the oleander bushes and tore at the wisteria vine Kate had trained with such patience, threatening to rip its tendrils from the eaves. The roiling clouds matched the stormy hue of Jeff Parrish's eyes.

Kate pattered down the hallway to her room, tossed the towel on the bed, and finger-combed the tangles out of her hair. Forget Jeff Parrish, she admonished herself. The man was a hopeless, hidebound snob, and she pitied any woman addlepated enough to give him a second glance.

As for his ridiculous family tradition—

A knock at the front door, faint but insistent, shattered her train of thought. Kate hesitated; then, remembering she'd remanded Flannery to her room, she knotted the sash on her robe and hurried down the hall. As she raced across the living room, the weak tapping, like the peck of a storm-tossed bird, grew more urgent, more frantic.

She flung open the door to find a small, forlorn figure trembling on the stoop.

"Ellen!" She swept the little girl inside. Jeff Parrish's daughter was wearing jeans and a pink T-shirt, all soaked with rain. Water dripped off the end of her nose and streamed down her hair to puddle on the floor.

Kate seized a knitted afghan off the couch and flung it around the shivering little body. There would be time for questions later. Right now she had to get the child warm and dry.

Racing back down the hall, she snatched an armful of towels from the bathroom shelf. She returned to find that Flannery had come out of her room. "Get Ellen some dry clothes," Kate ordered, letting the violation pass for now. "Something warm. Then, young lady, you've got some explaining to do!"

"Can Ellen stay here? Please—"

"Flannery, you're really pushing it!"

"I only drew her a map to our house," Flannery said. "I didn't know she'd be coming here tonight, in the rain."

"Go on," Kate sighed. "Get the clothes. We'll deal with what you did later." She took the thickest towel and began blotting rainwater from Ellen's long, black hair. The child's father and grandmother were probably frantic. As soon as she got Ellen dried off, Kate resolved, she would hurry to the phone and call them.

Ellen had begun to respond to the warm blanket and vigorous toweling. The color had returned to her cheeks. Her shy, gray eyes explored the room, lingering on the plump, orange tabby curled among the sofa cushions.

"What's his name?" she asked, her teeth still chattering a little.

"*Her* name. It's Mehitabel. She's named after a cat in a book of poems."

"Can I pet her?"

"As soon as you're dried off." Kate tugged the neck of

the soggy, pink T-shirt over Ellen's ears. "I don't suppose your father knows where you are, does he?"

Ellen shook her head, rosebud lips pressed tightly together as the shirt pulled free of her head. Her eyes, when she looked at Kate, were large with wonder.

"Are you...the clown?"

Kate chuckled in spite of herself. "That's right, dear. This is the real me. Or maybe it's Jo-Jo who's the real me. After a day like this one, I'm not so sure."

"And do *you* believe in mermaids?"

A warning flickered in Kate's mind. "I believe in the gift of imagination," she said, tucking the afghan around Ellen's bare chest and shoulders. "Hang on a sec, and I'll see if Flannery's found you some dry clothes. Then you can pet Mehitabel while I call your—"

The rap at the door was fierce and urgent. Kate froze, her mouth suddenly dry, her pulse jumping like a beached pompano. There was no need to wonder who was outside, or to question what was going through his mind. Any way you looked at it, the next few minutes were not bound to be pleasant.

Steeling herself for the confrontation to come, Kate squared her shoulders and marched across the room to answer the door.

Kate's house had not been difficult to find. Jeff remembered it, in fact, from the summers of his boyhood—a low-slung structure that clung to the rim of the beach, its clapboard exterior so weathered that the house looked more like an outsize hunk of driftwood than a dwelling place. An elderly man had lived here back then, Jeff recalled, a salty, reclusive old codger he'd often seen shuffling along the edge of the tide with his two mongrel dogs.

But never mind the past—it was Kate Valera who lived

here now. Through the drizzling curtain of rain, he could see her Jeep parked in the makeshift carport. He could see the faint glow of light through curtained windows—and as he raised his hand to knock again, Jeff could only hope to heaven she would know something about Ellen.

The door opened before his knuckles could strike again. The woman who stood before him, haloed by the lamplight behind her, was even smaller than he remembered. Her damp, reddish curls spilled around a sharp little fox face that seemed to be mostly eyes. Her hands tugged nervously at the sash of a thick green bathrobe that looked about four sizes too big for her.

"Ellen's here," she said calmly. "Come on in."

Jeff stepped across the threshold, dimly aware of the light and warmth that enfolded him as he did so. Relief jellied his knees as he spotted his daughter huddled in the corner of a flowered sofa, her arms embracing an immense, mustard-colored cat.

Fear dissolved into anger as he took a step toward her. "Young lady, do you have any idea what—"

"Please don't be mad, Daddy." Her sad-eyed gaze tore at his heart. "It's so lonesome in the house. There's nobody there but grown-ups. I just wanted to play with Flannery for a little while."

"And how did you know where to find Flannery?" Jeff demanded, but more gently this time. He knew how much his daughter needed a friend her own age. He'd seen it that afternoon, from the window.

"I can answer your question," Kate said. "Flannery drew her a map."

"So, Ellen just showed up on your doorstep in the rain?"

"Of course she did." Kate glared at him as if he'd just accused her of kidnapping. "I was about to phone your house when you knocked." She walked away a few steps, then turned to face him again. "And now that your daughter's safely found, I suppose you'll both be going."

Jeff's eyes measured her where she stood, poised like a gazelle beside an open cabinet that overflowed with books. Her small, square chin was thrust defiantly upward. Her eyes blazed wounded pride. Still hugging the cat, Ellen watched them in expectant silence.

No, Jeff realized, he couldn't be so monstrous as to grab his daughter and walk out. He couldn't do that to Ellen. He couldn't do it to Kate—or to himself.

"I—uh—think we need to talk," he muttered, suddenly aware that his clothes were dripping water onto her faded Persian rug.

"All right." Her body relaxed but her eyes remained guarded. "Flannery, dear, I know you're listening."

The child materialized from the hallway.

"Take Ellen to your bedroom for a little while, okay? And make sure you get her into something dry."

"*Yes!*" Flannery's grin lit the room like a flash bulb. "Come on, Ellen!" she exclaimed, bounding over to the couch. "You can wear my purple sweats, and I'll show you my sea glass collection!"

"Cool!" Ellen struggled off the sofa, clutching the afghan to her chest. "Can we take Mehitabel with us?"

"Sure." Flannery scooped up the cat. The placid creature hung over her arm like a limp Salvador Dali watch as the little girls scampered down the hallway, leaving the two grown-ups alone.

"Uh—can I make you some hot tea?" Kate spoke almost too swiftly as she scrambled to fill the awkward silence.

"No, that's all right." Jeff's gaze explored the room, taking in the lush, green jumble of houseplants, the seashells and driftwood, the varicolored cushions and worn, mismatched furniture, all of which blended, somehow, into an ambiance of cozy warmth. Outside, cold, gray rain lashed the roof and battered the windowpanes. Inside, the whole room seemed to glow.

"Well, we can sit down, at least," she said, settling onto a low ottoman. The neck of her robe had fallen open to reveal the luminous curve of her throat. Her skin was delicately freckled, like tiny dots of cinnamon sprinkled on rich cream. Jeff battled the ridiculous urge to bend over and taste her.

"I—my clothes are pretty wet," he muttered.

"Oh, sit down. You can't do anything to that couch that hasn't been done a hundred times before."

Jeff moved the cushions aside and lowered himself onto the threadbare upholstery. "Sorry about that. I drove over here, but before that, I was running along the beach like a wild man. I was afraid Ellen had tried to go back out to the rocks."

"You must have been frantic." Her aquamarine eyes were cautious.

"Out of my mind is more like it. Ellen's never done anything like this before. If she hadn't been here—"

"I know. But she *was* here. And she's fine—"

"What are we going to do about those two, Kate?" Jeff leaned toward her. His gaze probed hers, only to meet a solid barrier beyond which she would not allow him to go.

"If you're asking me how you can manage to keep your daughter in a glass box, safe from the lower classes and uncontaminated by anybody's ideas except your own—"

"Blast it, will you get that chip off your shoulder?" He exhaled sharply, fighting the impulse to reach out and grab the front of her robe. "I meant nothing of the sort. It's just that... Look, I realize Ellen is desperately lonely. She needs a friend, and she seems to have zeroed in on your daughter."

"In spite of your mother's efforts to find her some proper little chums."

"This isn't about my mother. And you're not making this any easier."

"I'm sorry, I didn't know I was supposed to." She uncoiled restlessly from the ottoman and walked to the window, where she parted the curtains and stood gazing out at the storm.

Seething, Jeff got up and crossed the room to stand behind her. For all his frustration, her nearness sparked quivers of sensual awareness in him. Her hair smelled of a delicate herbal soap. He found himself wondering how it would feel to bury his nose in her soft, damp curls or to tug back the collar of her robe and nuzzle the satiny nape of her neck.

Blast the woman!

Jerking his thoughts back to the matter at hand, he forced himself to speak. "Look, all I'm really trying to say is that if we can manage to keep them out of trouble, I'd like our daughters to be friends."

If he'd expected Kate to melt, he'd misjudged her. She stood with her back rigid, her head high, staring out at the rain. "You make it sound so simple," she said.

"Isn't it?"

She shook her head, refusing to turn and look at him. "Summer people like you—you come here for the season, you rent a house, you rent a boat and some fishing tackle, you rent a little friend to keep your child company—"

"Kate." He put his hands on her shoulders and turned her gently around to face him. Her eyes glittered with what could have been unshed tears or only reflected lamplight.

"You're concerned about your daughter," she said. "That's only right. But Flannery isn't your therapy tool. I don't want her to feel like a discarded plaything when the summer's over and Ellen goes back to Raleigh."

Something softened in Jeff as he gazed into her vulnerable, honest face. He struggled for an answer, not finding it until he heard squeals of childish laughter from the room down the hall. "Listen," he said. "It's not complicated to them. Why should it be so complicated to us?"

He felt her hesitate. "And what about the mermaids?" she asked.

"I'll deal with the mermaids in my own way."

"Daddy, look!" Ellen burst into the room, her eyes dancing like Fourth of July sparklers. The long-suffering cat dangled over her arm wearing a bonnet and a ruffled pink doll dress. "Look at Mehitabel! She's going to a party! Isn't she beautiful?"

Jeff rolled his eyes toward the ceiling. Kate choked on an ill-suppressed giggle. "I think we could all use some nice, hot soup," she said. "I can have it warmed up in about five minutes!"

Jeff had expected, maybe, Campbell's Chicken Noodle. But he had underestimated Kate Valera. The soup was a savory homemade concoction of carrots, leeks, potatoes, barley and a mélange of mouth-watering flavors he could not have begun to name. It was accompanied by thick slices of whole wheat bread with butter and a big bowl of fresh, tossed salad greens. Even Ellen, a fussy nibbler at home, dug in and ate heartily.

Jeff's gaze followed Kate across the kitchen as she flitted up from the table to refill the pepper mill. She had replaced her robe with faded jeans and a black ballet-style cotton sweater. Her trim little body moved like a dancer's, with an easy, mesmerizing grace.

"Say when." She leaned around him to grind fresh pepper on his salad. Her breast brushed the tip of his ear, sending an erotic jolt all the way to Jeff's knees. The fork he'd been holding clattered to the table. He retrieved it quietly, hoping she wouldn't notice.

"Enough?" The rasp of her sexy little voice sent an electric pulse along his nerve endings.

Enough? Not nearly enough, lady.

"Uh—yes, that's fine," he managed to respond, eyeing the abundant black pepper specks on the dark green leaves. "Thanks."

"I know how Ellen got here," she said, slipping back into her chair. "But I still can't figure out how you found this place."

"You left your duffel—it's in my trunk." Jeff relaxed a little as the conversation moved on to safe ground. "The address was scratched inside the lid of your makeup box, so I took a chance. But I can't help wondering who Frank Valera is. I, uh, don't see him anywhere."

"Frank Valera was my grandfather." Kate nibbled at her salad. "He died ten years ago and left me this house and everything in it, including the duffel bag—oh, and thank you for finding it. I confess I hadn't even missed it. I'm afraid I took off in something of a rush—must've assumed it was in the Jeep."

"I'll bring it in before I leave," said Jeff. "Oh, and one more thing. Your offer to give your show free of charge was very generous, but it wasn't necessary. I'll drop by the agency tomorrow and—"

"No!" Kate's eyes flashed like barricade flares. "The show was a fiasco from start to finish. I caused no end of trouble. I transformed Muffet Bodell into a clown, I upset your mother—"

"You were magnificent," Jeff said, meaning it.

"Sure." She shot him a withering glance.

"Hey—I caught your act from the window. Those kids were a tough audience, but you *had* them. And you certainly deserve to be paid for—"

"No." The quiet finality in her voice told Jeff that more arguing would be wasted effort. "All I want from this afternoon is to slink off with my dignity intact."

She bent to finishing her soup with a resolve that closed a door between them. Jeff sat watching her for the space of a long breath, aching to open it again. The compelling glimpses he'd caught of Kate Valera only heightened the intrigue, whetting his desire to see, touch and know more. She was like an exquisite little jigsaw puzzle, offering him no more than one tantalizing piece at a time.

"Flannery's writing a book, Daddy." Ellen piped into the silence. "It's all about mermaids. She says I can read it anytime I want to."

Jeff resolved to be polite. "So, Flannery, how long is your book going to be?" he asked.

"So far it's filled four and a half notebooks." Flannery's long eyes were hazel, almost ginger, with a fey intelligence glittering in their depths. In old-time Salem, such a child might have been burned as a witch.

"I don't know how many more notebooks it will take," she continued. "Mom says I'll need to type the whole thing before I send it to a publisher. If she sells enough pots this summer, we're going to buy ourselves a computer."

"Sells enough pots?" Jeff recalled Kate mentioning her pottery studio, but not much more.

"I've got my work in a few galleries around town," Kate said. "Things are picking up. If I can expand into some of the big cities, I'll be able to sell year-round instead of depending on summers."

"And then maybe you won't have to wait tables at the Pancake Palace anymore," Flannery said. "Right, Mom?"

"Uh, right." Kate glanced down at her empty soup bowl. "Hey, everybody seems to be finished. Who'd like some fresh raspberry shortcake?"

"Me!" Ellen and Flannery piped in unison.

"How about you?" She glanced at Jeff across the table.

"None for me, thanks." His mind scrambled for another piece of the puzzle. "But, you know, I'd really like to see some of your work before I take Ellen home."

"There are a few finished pieces in my studio." Kate was on her feet now, filling two saucers with cake, berries and squirts of whipped cream. "I can show you while the girls are finishing their dessert."

"Thanks. I'd like that." Jeff savored a prickle of anticipation as he followed her out of the kitchen. Not that he was any great connoisseur of pottery. His interest in the art form was casual at best. But his interest in Kate Valera was simmering rapidly to a fever pitch. Instinct warned him to be cautious, but Jeff wasn't buying the message. He wanted more pieces of the puzzle.

"This is my studio." Kate flipped on the light in the garage she'd converted six years ago. Even though she'd done nearly all of the work herself, it had been an expensive project, insulating the walls, plumbing in a sink and a gas line for her kiln, building the counters and shelves. The old garage still didn't look like much, but at least she had a year-round place to work.

Jeff Parrish stood in the doorway gazing disdainfully down his gorgeously scrunched nose. As an architect, he was obviously not impressed with her studio. She could scarcely blame him. But she was proud of what she'd created inside these four walls, and no one could take that away from her.

"My finished pots are on that far shelf. This way,

please.'' She ushered him around the clutter of her large kick-based wheel, around covered storage vats and fifty-pound bags of dry clay. "Watch your clothes," she said. "This is a messy place."

"My clothes?" Only when he laughed did Kate remember that he was wet and muddy from the rain. She liked his laugh—liked the way the deep *ha!* burst out of him, as if it had broken through the seams of his straight-laced exterior. Maybe there was more to Jeff Parrish than the superior scowl she'd judged to be his permanent expression.

She stopped in front of a tall shelf. "These three pieces were fired last week. I haven't had time to take them around to the galleries yet. Take a look."

She stepped back a little, holding her breath. It shouldn't matter what this man thought of her craft, Kate reminded herself. All the same, as his gaze traveled over the massive, coiled Raku bowl, the three-foot-high, salt-glazed urn with its matching lid and the intricately incised stoneware lantern, she found herself desperately wanting him to like what he saw. It was almost as if she were showing him pieces of her soul.

"You don't exactly work small, do you?" he said after what seemed like an eternal silence.

"No, I don't." Kate struggled to ignore a stab of disappointment. "As I told you, I make gallery pieces. They're not scaled for your average coffee table."

"I realize that—but in terms of sheer practicality, wouldn't you sell more if you made at least some of your pieces smaller and more affordable?"

"I...suppose so." She hesitated, then turned on him, eyes blazing with the fire his words had touched off inside her.

"It's not a question of practicality," she snapped. "It's a question of—of passion!"

"Passion?" His eyes flickered skeptically.

"This work—these pots—I do them with my heart, not my head. Don't you see? If I were to let practicality interfere with what I love, I'd lose it all. The love, the passion—"

"Kate Valera, you're a beautiful piece of work," he said.

She glared at him, smarting with irritation.

"I'll tell you what," he said. "Do you have photos of your work? I know a couple of gallery owners in Raleigh who might be interested. I'd be glad to send the pictures around and put in a good word for you."

"You'd really do that?" She blinked at him, thrown off balance by his surprising offer.

"I'd be honored. Especially if it would help get you free of the Pancake Palace."

"Oh, that." Kate's spirit sagged again as the possibility sank home that he was patronizing her. "It's no big deal. Just something I do during the school year while Flannery's in class. Summers I try to keep her with me while I peddle pottery, do Jo-Jo and teach a yoga class five mornings a week at the health club. It's all in the name of—"

"Of passion?"

Her breath caught as his gaze crept through her like a warm, spring tide. "I was going to say survival," she murmured, her knees going soft beneath her. "But passion will do as well. Why are you looking at me that way?"

"Because I just realized this is no time and place for a long conversation." His voice carried an edge, a husky little burr that shimmered through her body like the stroke of a feather. "Have dinner with me, Kate. Tomorrow night, if you're free. We've got a lot to talk about."

"Such as?" The thought that he was just feeding her a line lent a raw edge to Kate's retort.

"You could tell me more about your work. We could discuss setting some limits for our daughters—"

"I don't leave Flannery alone at night."

"She could stay with Ellen at my house. What do you say?"

"Mom!" Flannery came bounding into the studio. "Can Ellen sleep over tonight?"

"No!" Kate snatched at her daughter's question like a passing life preserver. "You two have gotten into enough mischief for one day."

"Run and tell Ellen I'll be taking her home in a minute." Jeff bent his head toward Kate. "Hey, it's just dinner," he muttered in her ear. "And the girls can have a sleepover at my place. Come on, what have you got to lose?"

She hesitated, knowing better.

"Kate?" The note of vulnerability in his voice was just subtle enough. His chin grazed her hair, sending a tingling response along each strand.

"Oh—all right, why not?" she heard herself saying as her slamming pulse threw her judgment out of whack. Even if he *could* get her work noticed in Raleigh, she knew she was stepping into a quagmire.

"Seven-thirty?"

"Seven-thirty's fine." Yes, she had truly lost her mind.

"Hang on, I'll grab your duffel."

He hurried ahead of her into the house, leaving Kate to turn off the light in the studio. Her hand paused, trembling, on the switch.

It would be all right, she reassured herself. Just a casual, pleasant dinner, and maybe—just maybe—a chance to promote her work. If Jeff Parrish could interest some gallery owners in her pottery, the possibilities were...

But who was she kidding? She was already in deep trouble. Jefferson Parrish III was one of the most compellingly attractive men she had ever met, and his interest in her, she sensed, had nothing to do with her pottery.

He was a one-way ticket to heartbreak.

Jeff Parrish was what Misty Point's year-round residents would call a summer man—a seasonal visitor, wealthy and cultured, who might divert himself for a few weeks with a local girl, maybe turn her head with a few expensive gifts and heady promises. But that was all. The end of the story was always the same.

Kate knew about summer men. She knew them all too well.

She wandered back into the kitchen and began clearing the table, rinsing the dishes and stacking them in the sink to be washed. Outside, the sounds of the storm had faded to a gentle patter.

"We're leaving now." Jeff's husky frame filled the doorway. "Your bag's inside. Thanks for everything, Kate. I'll see you tomorrow night."

"See you." Kate turned away, squirted some detergent into the dishpan and turned on the faucet full force. She heard him cross the living room, heard the girls saying good-night.

Snatching up a plastic scrubber, she attacked the dishes with a vengeance born of desperation. What kind of fool was she? What kind of mistake had she made, opening her life to Jeff Parrish and his lonely little daughter? Should she break and run, or was it already too late?

She was still asking questions when Jeff's car pulled out of the driveway and disappeared into the rainy twilight.

Chapter Four

Kate pulled the Jeep into the carport and collapsed against the worn canvas upholstery. A wave of soggy summer heat had followed last night's rain, and the air was like simmering chicken soup. Worse, she had spent the past seven hours as Jo-Jo, entertaining kids in the asphalt parking lot of a new toy store. Beneath the padded clown suit, her body felt like a sweat-shriveled prune. Her feet were swollen tender lumps.

Worst of all, her dinner date with Jeff Parrish was only an hour away.

"Can Mehitabel come to Ellen's house with me?" Flannery clambered out of the Jeep, impervious to the wilting heat. "Please… Ellen likes her!"

Kate groaned as she unglued her aching body from the seat. "No, Mehitabel can't go. Cats don't enjoy sleepovers. Besides, somebody has to stay here and guard the house against pirates and ghosts—"

"And wicked sea demons!" Flannery giggled. "Mehitabel is good at that! She turns them into mice with a flick of her magic tail, and then she eats them for supper!'' She performed an eager little jig on the stoop as she waited for her mother to catch up and unlock the door. ''Can I take Ellen one of our conch shells?''

''I'm sure that would be fine.'' Kate dragged her body into the living room, reasoning that even the Picky Parrishes, as she'd begun to think of them, could not possibly object to such a simple gift. ''Choose the prettiest one on the shelf. And while you're at it, make sure you pack your toothbrush and some pajamas in your overnight bag.''

''The blue ones with the flying toasters?'' Flannery bounded across the living room like a carrot-topped gazelle.

''Are they clean?''

''Uh-huh.''

''Fine, then.'' Kate dumped the heavy duffel behind the couch. ''If you need the bathroom, hurry. I've got to shower, and there's not much time.''

''I'm okay. I went at the toy store.'' Flannery headed down the hallway, hesitated, then turned around. ''You know, Mom, if you married Ellen's dad, then Ellen and I could be sisters.''

Kate stumbled over the rug, slamming her knee into a corner of the bookshelf. Her breath exploded in a whoosh of pain. ''Flannery Valera, I don't know what put such a crazy notion into your head!'' she sputtered.

Flannery shrugged. ''He likes you. He asked you out to dinner. And you're going.''

''I'm going out to dinner with Jeff Parrish because he might be able to connect me with some gallery owners in Raleigh. That certainly doesn't mean I'd be fool enough to think of marrying him!''

''Not even if he asked you?''

''He would never ask me, sweetheart. And even if he did, I would never say yes.''

"Why not?"

Because men like Jeff Parrish don't marry women like me. Kate bit back the words, but she could not suppress the thought.

"Mom?" Flannery was still waiting for an answer.

"We're...very different, that's all. Remember 'The Little Mermaid'?"

"The movie or the real story?"

"The real story. The one by Hans Christian Andersen. What happened when the Little Mermaid grew legs and tried to be somebody she wasn't?"

"She died." Flannery's face sobered as the message sank home. "She died, and the prince married somebody else."

"Exactly." Kate ripped open the Velcro strip that held the front of her costume together and used a handy sale circular to fan her dripping chest. "She should have stayed in the ocean where she belonged. She could have married some nice young merman and had some cute little merbabies and lived a long, happy life—"

"Are you saying you ought to marry somebody like Howard Bangerter?"

"I'm not saying I should marry anyone!" Kate knew that the owner of the Pancake Palace was interested in dating her, but so far she'd managed to keep him at arm's length. Howard Bangerter was a nice enough fellow, but he wasn't her type.

Jefferson Parrish, unfortunately, was.

"But, Mom—"

"You're pushing it, Flannery," she said. "Run along to your room, now. I've got to jump in the shower."

Kate's daughter obeyed—for about three skips. Then she turned around and strode back into the living room, a determined expression fixed on her sharp little freckled face.

"Ellen's dad isn't a prince," she said. "He's just a sad, lonely man, that's what Ellen says. And I can tell he likes you a lot."

"Flannery…" Kate's voice carried an undertone of menace.

"I'm going!" She flashed out of sight, leaving Kate to stumble into the bathroom, close the door, and strip out of the sweltering Jo-Jo costume.

In the shower she closed her eyes and let the blissfully cool water sluice over her skin. If she had any sense, she would telephone the Parrish house and call the whole thing off, she lectured herself. Certainly it would be nice to sell her work in Raleigh, maybe gain some exposure that would lead to bigger and better things. But was it worth the risk of making a fool of herself and getting her heart kicked around in the bargain?

Was it worth the risk of hurting Flannery?

Disgusted with her own weakness, she squeezed out some shampoo and lathered her hair to a bubbly froth. Just this one date and nothing more, she vowed. She would have a nice, businesslike dinner with Jeff Parrish. They would exchange polite conversation over a good meal. Then she would make her excuses and bid him an early good-night.

What had possessed her, agreeing to let Flannery stay overnight with Ellen? Her most plausible excuse for an early exit was already out the window!

Kate could feel her nervous tension growing as she stepped out of the shower, toweled herself dry and splashed on some of the Emeraude body cologne Flannery had given her for Christmas. A glance at the little porcelain clock on the nightstand told her she had twenty minutes to finish getting ready.

Twenty minutes. And Jeff Parrish, she knew, would not

be late. The man probably brushed his teeth and blew his nose on a set schedule!

Deodorant—she fanned her underarms to dry the gooey liquid while she stared into her closet with a looming sense of hopelessness. She had nothing to wear. The little black number with the spaghetti straps was much too suggestive. The beige linen suit would look like an unmade bed by the time she got out of the car. The navy blue PTA outfit with the white collar—no, definitely not.

With time running out, she settled on a sleeveless jade green silk dress she'd had for more years than she cared to remember. The flared, knee-length skirt was short by current fashion standards, but the color flattered her fair skin and brought out the subtle green flecks in her eyes. Saks Fifth Avenue it wasn't, but it would have to do.

Flinging the dress on the bed, she hurried back to the bathroom where she finger-combed some mousse into her curls. She returned to find Mehitabel reclining like an odalisque on the rumpled jade silk.

"Shoo!" Kate hissed impatiently. "Off with you! I need my dress!"

The cat stared at her with baleful amber eyes, refusing to move.

Kate sighed. "All right, Mehitabel. I know you're trying to save me from my own folly. But I'm a big girl. Trust me, I can handle a single evening with a rich, gorgeous, lonesome hunk without losing my head."

Mehitabel sniffed disdainfully and flexed a hooked claw into the delicate fabric. She was an old cat, older than Flannery, and not one to be intimidated by a mere human.

"Oh, no, you don't!" Kate scooped one hand under the ample, feline belly and used her other hand to free the obstinate claw. "I realize you watched me make a mess of my life once, but trust me, I'm on top of this one. I know who I am. I know who he is, and I'm too smart to let myself get kicked around again.''

Mehitabel's only response was a skeptical *meowwr* as Kate hoisted her gently off the dress and deposited her among the cushions piled at the head of the bed.

"Okay, so you don't believe me,'' Kate muttered. "Smart thinking, old girl. I'm not so sure that *I* believe me, either. But I've got to keep my wits about me tonight, or I'm in deep yogurt!''

The cat fluffed her tangerine fur and closed her eyes as Kate shook out the dress and tugged it over her head. Stay calm, she admonished herself. But it was useless advice, she realized as she worked tiny rhinestone studs into her pierced ears. She felt like Cinderella dressing for the ball, with the clock already racing toward midnight.

Her heart, she realized, was racing with it.

Jeff swallowed a tingle of anticipation as he pulled into Kate's driveway and parked behind the Jeep. There was no need to be nervous, he reminded himself. Beyond dinner and conversation, the evening promised nothing. As for his partner, he had dated more glamorous women than Kate Valera—more elegant, more polished and certainly more socially daunting. Kate was an intriguing cipher, a feisty little fish in a small, backwater pond, Jeff reminded himself. He had nothing to fear from her.

So why did he feel as jittery as a high school freshman on his first prom date?

"Can I come inside?'' Ellen bounced up and down in the back of the BMW, straining against her seat belt.

"Flannery should be out any minute.''

"Please. I want to see Mehitabel.''

"Okay. But behave yourself.'' Jeff opened the back door, grateful for the moment that his daughter had come along. Maybe it would ease the awkwardness, starting out with both girls along.

He strode up the walk, but Ellen danced ahead of him to ring the front bell—which was just as well, because it was Flannery who opened the door. The two little girls greeted each other by bouncing up and down like miniature Watusi dancers before Kate's daughter remembered her manners.

"Mom will be out in a second," she said, her sharp ginger eyes dissecting Jeff's casual gray polo shirt, navy blue chinos and tan linen jacket. "She looks beautiful, just like a fairy princess."

"I'm sure she does." Jeff felt like a bug under a magnifying glass. He shifted his feet awkwardly, wishing he'd worn a tie. This fey, insightful child, he sensed, did not approve of him or his evening wear.

"Please, may I see your cat?" Ellen's eager question came as a relief. The two little girls skipped off down the hall, leaving Jeff alone in the living room.

Restless, he prowled the faded Persian carpet, turning one way, then another. His gaze roamed the cluttered shelves, lingering on the trailing green philodendrons, seashells and driftwood, dog-eared volumes of poetry and a whimsical terra-cotta mermaid that could only be Kate's work. The lower shelves held more books—ragged, time-worn children's classics. *Grimm's Fairy Tales, The Wizard of Oz, The Chronicles of Narnia...* Jeff scanned the titles, realizing he had not read even one of them. Fluff and babble, his father would have called such books. Nonsensical time wasters, good for nothing but to delude reason and dull the mind.

Maybe that was so, Jeff mused. But there was certainly nothing dull about Kate Valera.

A bright flicker caught his eye. Curious, he picked up a

miniature glass unicorn from the top shelf and balanced it on his palm. The long, spiraling horn, as delicate as a needle, sparkled with reflected light. Such a fragile little thing, he mused; if he so much as closed his fingers around it, it would shatter like a—

"Hello."

Kate's husky voice went through him like wind through long, summer grass. Jeff's breath caught as he turned around. The tiny ornament toppled from his hand, bounced off a corner of the shelf and broke into myriad splinters of glass.

"Oh, no—blast it, I'm sorry..." Jeff bent forward at the same time she did, and they bumped heads with a force that left him dizzy. "Here," he muttered, reddening. "Let me—"

"No, you'll cut yourself. I'll get the Dustbuster."

She flitted toward the kitchen, leaving Jeff to curse his own clumsiness. Their date—or whatever it ought to be called—was not off to an auspicious beginning.

He gazed down at the scattered fragments, thinking that the little ornament must have meant something to Kate, or she would not have kept it in such a high, safe place. How could it have happened? Jeff asked himself. How could he have managed to do such an oafish thing?

His mind flew back to the instant before he dropped the unicorn. He had thrilled to the sound of Kate's voice, then turned around to see her standing there in a dress that clung heartstoppingly to her lush little figure and made blue-green flames of her eyes. What in blazes had happened to him then? Had he been so stunned by the sight of her that he'd lost his wits?

Kate returned with the Dustbuster and began vacuuming up the glass. Jeff watched her, feeling incompetent and foolish.

"I'll pay you for it," he said.

"Don't be silly." There was a rough little catch to her voice. "It was nothing but a worthless trinket."

"But I had no business touching it."

"That's right, you didn't. But what's done is done." She had turned off the machine and was staring fixedly at the floor. For the space of a long breath, neither of them spoke.

"Kate..."

When she did not answer, he bent down and captured her chin with the tip of his finger. With a gently coaxing motion, he tilted her face to the light.

Her eyes were brimming with tears.

At that moment Jeff would have donned a suit of armor and galloped to her rescue. He would have fought fire-breathing dragons, scaled mountains of ice, vanquished twenty-foot giants—anything to erase those tears.

"Dammit, I'm sorry—" he murmured.

"Don't."

Her eyes flashed a warning, but he was beyond its heeding. Never in his life had Jefferson Parrish III felt a more compelling urge to kiss a woman.

Hungering for the warm honey silk of her mouth, he leaned closer, and—

"Let's go, Daddy! We're all ready!" Ellen frisked into the living room with Flannery at her heels, shattering the magic like a rainbow bubble.

Jeff's reason returned and he drew back from the spell of Kate's heady aura. Almost instantly, he was grateful for the interruption. He had already made one faux pas tonight. The last thing he needed was to make another. Kate Valera was a tempting morsel, but taking her in his arms would have meant stepping into emotional quicksand. He was not ready to take that kind of risk—especially after making up his mind that the next time he got involved with a woman, his head, not his hormones, would rule the choices he made.

Besides, Jeff rationalized, he respected Kate too much to start a game he had no intention of finishing. Tonight would be business, nothing more. Over dinner they would discuss Kate's work and come to an agreement about supervising their daughters' time together. That done, they would shake hands and bid each other a civilized good-night.

Flannery was lugging a loaded backpack and a rolled sleeping bag toward the door. Without asking, Jeff lifted them out of her arms, strode outside to the BMW, and tossed them into the trunk. "Come on, everybody, let's get going!" he announced to the blue twilight, and was relieved when the girls responded, skipping and giggling down the driveway to tumble into the back seat.

Everything was under control and would remain so, Jeff reassured himself as he opened the passenger door for Kate. But as she slid past him, her silk skirt swishing against his legs, a surge of desire hit him so hard that he almost moaned out loud.

Tonight, he realized, would not be as easy as he'd hoped. If he lowered his guard with Kate Valera for so much as a heartbeat, he would be in big trouble.

And trouble, in the guise of a spunky, vulnerable little redhead, was looking sweeter by the minute.

At the Parrish cottage, which loomed through the twilight mist like an apparition out of *The Great Gatsby*, Jeff escorted the girls inside. Kate opted to stay in the car. Granted, it was a cowardly decision, but she did not feel up to facing Jeff's dragonly mother. Not tonight.

She sat with the window down, letting the sea wind cool her hot face. Her fingers alternately bunched and smoothed the folds of her skirt. She had overdressed—one look at

Jeff's casual attire had told her that much. Not that it really mattered. Nothing about tonight mattered. Nothing, that is, except getting through the evening with her dignity intact.

In her mind she saw the little glass unicorn again, lying shattered on the faded maroon carpet. She'd been a sentimental fool, letting herself get weepy over it. Jeff Parrish had done her a favor, she told herself. She should have thrown the bauble away years ago—and would have done so, except for the chance that one day it might mean something to Flannery. Now that it was gone, she felt a curious sense of passage, as if a gate had closed behind her.

"Hello again." Jeff's voice startled her out of her reverie. He opened the door on the driver's side of the car and eased his solid, muscular body into the seat, bringing with him the subtle aroma of expensive sandalwood soap. "I think I got the girls settled in," he said. "They should be fine. Mother said she rented some *National Geographic* videos for them to watch."

"What? No Disney?"

"Careful, your chip is showing."

"What?"

"I'm talking about the chip on your shoulder." He flashed her a sidelong grin as he switched on the lights and ignition. Purring like a cheetah, the sleek silver car glided out of the driveway.

Kate forced herself to return his smile as she settled back against the baby-soft leather upholstery. There was no law against being civil, she reminded herself. But when she groped for a charming, witty retort, she fumbled and came up empty. This evening was going to be one long chain of mistakes.

"I hope tonight isn't too much of an imposition on your mother," she said lamely.

"Mother will be fine. All she has to do is sit back and let the girls entertain each other."

"But I don't think she approves of Flannery. She certainly doesn't approve of me. Not that it should matter one way or the other—"

"Relax, it'll be all right." He swung the car onto the main road and eased down on the accelerator. "I thought we might go to The Cove," he said. "They've got great blue crab, and the swordfish isn't bad, either. Does that sound okay?"

"Uh-huh." Kate tried to appear unimpressed, even though The Cove was a restaurant for the summer people, so pricey that she had never even set foot inside the door. "Anyplace is fine," she said, brushing tense fingers through her still-damp curls. "As long as it isn't the Pancake Palace."

His husky laugh curled in her ear, tingling like a caress through her quivering senses. She cast covert glances at his rugged profile, silhouetted by the same moon that silvered his thick, flawlessly cut hair. If only he were ugly, she thought. If only he were dull or crude or swollen with self-importance. Then the evening would hold no fears for her. She could be charmingly detached then, full of wit and humor, knowing that her heart was safe.

As it was, Kate felt as if her heart were balancing on a tightrope over a shark-infested whirlpool.

"What the devil did your daughter have in that backpack of hers?" Jeff's eyes caught a glimmer of moonlight as he glanced her way.

Kate blinked at him. "She was supposed to pack her pajamas, her toothbrush and a seashell for Ellen. Why?"

"When I picked it up, it was heavy. Must've weighed ten or fifteen... Good Lord, I hope it wasn't your cat! My mother can't abide cats. They give her asthma."

Kate slumped in her seat with a groan, remembering Flannery's request to take Mehitabel to Ellen's house. She remembered, too, her last sight of the placid, orange cat curled among the cushions on her bed. Would Mehitabel stand for being stuffed into a child's backpack? It seemed unlikely, but one never knew what Flannery could accomplish, and the possibility jabbed at Kate's mind like a persistent mosquito.

"Shouldn't we go back and check on them?" she asked anxiously.

Jeff hesitated, then sighed and shook his head. "What's done is done. Let's go ahead and enjoy our evening. Whatever's happening back there, we can deal with it later." He shifted into low and turned the car down the side road that led to the posh beachfront restaurant. "By the way, did I mention that you look stunning tonight?"

"Thank you," Kate muttered lamely, knowing the trite compliment was nothing more than a line. She did not look stunning. She looked…gaudy, she realized. Like a Christmas tree in July. She should have gone with the beige linen suit, wrinkles and all.

She stared straight ahead as Jeff swung into the parking lot and pulled up next to a sleek green Mercedes. Tiny electric lanterns danced in the shadows, illuminating clumps of glossy tropical foliage—imported, like the people.

"I remember this stretch of beach from the old days," she said as Jeff opened her car door. "I used to help my grandfather dig clams along here when the tide was low. It was beautiful then, so wild and clean."

"I know what it was like." He waited for Kate to accept his proffered arm. Through the soft linen of his sleeve, his flesh was as hard as oak. "As a boy, I used to sail my ketch around that point and anchor it in the cove to swim. I remember..." His breath caught as he stared at her. "It was you! The old man on the beach with the little red-haired girl—"

"And you—that boy." The recollection struck Kate like a flash of summer lightning. "You always came alone. I remember watching you dive off the stern. Sometimes you stayed under for so long I feared you might not come up—"

"I used to practice holding my breath underwater. I wanted to be an ocean explorer like Jacques Cousteau."

"What happened?" The unease between them had vanished for the moment. Chatting, they strolled across the parking lot and up the front steps of the restaurant.

"Practicality took over," he said. "I showed a flair for design, and my father decided I should go into architecture."

Kate stared at him, her lips parted in amazement. A hot little spark of indignation began to smolder inside her, fueled by the notion that this man had never needed to reach for anything in his life. It had all been handed to him, on a polished silver platter.

And the worst of it was, he didn't seem to care.

"Your *father* decided?" Her voice echoed her disbelief.

Jeff shrugged offhandedly. "Oh, he didn't insist on it, mind you. But he nudged me in that direction. It was a good call. I've achieved a decent reputation in the field and managed to make a respectable living—"

"A decent reputation! A respectable living!" Kate burst out, forgetting her determination to enjoy a polite, civilized dinner date. "That's all well and good, but would you have fought for your creative life as an architect, Jeff Parrish? Does it fulfill you? Does it give you—"

"Passion?" His eyes glinted sardonically. "My dear

Kate, I'm not at all sure that anything gives me passion these days.''

Kate's jaw dropped, but the appearance of a silver-haired maître d' in a black tuxedo saved her the challenge of coming up with a fitting retort. Biting back her outrage, she followed the man to a secluded table, immaculately set with dark blue linens, white china and sparkling goblets. A single perfect yellow rose bloomed in a faceted crystal vase.

She kept her silence, avoiding Jeff's eyes as she slipped into her chair. The restaurant was crowded with diners, most of them lean and bronzed, dressed in chic summer-pale linens and khakis.

No, Kate reflected darkly, she did not belong here, not in this place, and certainly not with this man.

Jeff was scowling at his menu. "I believe I mentioned that the crabs are good here," he said, "as well as the swordfish.''

"I'll have the Caesar salad with a side of pasta," Kate said. "I'm sorry, I should have told you. I'm a vegetarian.''

"Another one of your passions, Kate Valera?" One black eyebrow had slithered upward, giving his square, tanned face an engagingly lopsided expression. How could such a maddening man be so irresistible? Kate wondered.

"Not a passion. Just a longtime habit," she said. "Now it's my turn to ask a question. How did you break that splendid nose of yours, and why didn't you get it fixed? The money could hardly have been an obstacle.''

He stared at her, then chuckled at her directness. "I wish I had an exciting story to tell you, but the truth is, I broke it playing rugby at Princeton. And I didn't get it fixed because this girl on the cheerleading squad remarked that it made me look tough. Would you care for some wine?''

"I love wine, but it makes me goofy," Kate said.

"I'd like to see you goofy." He nodded to the hovering

waiter, who appeared to be familiar with his preferences. The sparkling golden liquid swirled into Kate's glass before she had time to blink.

"All right, it's my turn again," he said, pausing to savor a sip from his glass. "Tell me about your passion. How did you come to be a maker of beautiful, giant-sized pots? Where did you learn?"

"I learned every way I could—took community education classes, read books, worked my hands pruney every night...." Kate could feel herself talking too fast. She took a tiny swallow of the dry, white wine. It tingled a warm path down her throat and set off shimmering bubble bursts in her head. "The first time I put my hands to clay, I knew I wanted to be a potter," she said, talking even faster. "I fell in love with the creative process of shaping and glazing and firing—of seeing the finished pot, and knowing it was mine. The whole thing—I know how corny this must sound, but it absolutely consumes me. Aside from Flannery, it's—yes, it's the most important thing in my life."

"And that's passion." An amused smile played at the corners of his beautifully chiseled mouth. "I envy you your passion, Kate. It becomes you."

"But don't you see?" A second sip of the wine had loosened her tongue even more. She was uncorked now, the words bubbling out of her without restraint. "This thing you call passion—you can have it, too. Anybody can. All it takes is putting your heart and soul into something you truly care about."

"Or *someone,* perhaps?" He was leaning back in his chair, playing with the stem of his glass. He was playing with her, as well, Kate realized.

"Some*thing* is generally safer. Some*ones* tend to disappear from your life at the worst possible times."

"What happened to Flannery's father, Kate?"

The question caught her off guard, like an unexpected slap. Her lips parted, then closed in stubborn silence.

"The little glass unicorn," he said, "the one I so clumsily dropped. It was from him, wasn't it?"

"So what if it was?" She stared down into her glass. "Things didn't work out between us. Even that is more than you need to know. Now, could we please talk about something else?"

"Of course, if you like."

Silence hung between them like a thick glass curtain. Kate squirmed wretchedly on her chair, groping for something intelligent to say and coming up empty. Her eyes searched the room in the frantic hope that the waiter would appear with their dinner entrées, but he was nowhere in sight.

She swirled the wine in her glass, feeling like an overdressed, tongue-tied fool. She'd hoped the evening would turn out pleasantly, at least, but that was not to be the case. The situation had already gone from awkward to uncomfortable.

Now, she sensed, it was approaching disastrous.

Chapter Five

Jeff studied Kate across the gulf of the table, wishing he could replay the last two minutes and take back his rash invasion of her past. He had craved another piece of the puzzle, another clue as to what made this haunting little woman the person she was. But in grasping for it, he had clearly blundered into forbidden territory. Once again he felt like an insensitive brute.

She looked so vulnerable sitting there in the candlelight, her restless, blunt-nailed fingers slowly twirling the stem of her wineglass. What kind of man would hurt a woman the way Kate Valera had so obviously been hurt? Jeff wondered. Had her husband been abusive? Had he been unfaithful? Had he deserted her?

She stirred restlessly under his gaze. "A penny for your thoughts," she said, her voice a feather's brush across his aroused senses.

"I was thinking about…passion," he said, mentally excusing the half lie.

She took the smallest sip of wine. "About passion? Or about your lack of it?"

"Ouch!"

"Don't 'ouch' me. You're the one who said it." The spark in her eyes, snuffed out by his mention of Flannery's father, had begun to flicker again. Encouraged, Jeff leaned forward in his chair, watching her in secret fascination.

"You obviously think there's something wrong with me," he said. "Suppose you tell me what it is."

Her eyes shot darts of exasperation. "Look at you, Jefferson Parrish!" she exclaimed. "You're no ordinary person! You're an architect! You create monuments, habitations—"

"So?" He was gently needling her now, playing devil's advocate and enjoying it.

"That day at the house—you said you had work to do. What kind of work was it?"

"I'm designing a new wing for a hospital in Raleigh."

"And that doesn't excite you?" Her eyes were incredulous aquamarine pools. "Think of all that goes on in a hospital, the drama, the battles between life and death—"

"It might excite me. Except that my creation has to fit the budget constraints, satisfy the hospital board and be filtered through three different committees. It's hard to get excited about any design conservative enough to run that kind of gauntlet and survive."

"I see." She glanced down at her hands, lost, for the moment, in a fury of thought. Jeff's eyes traced the contours of her cheekbones, lingering on the delicate splash of freckles that crossed her nose. Kate Valera was not the most beautiful woman he had ever known, but the play of emotions that flickered across her face was like dancing flame, pure and true and alive.

"Have you ever read *The Fountainhead?*" she asked suddenly.

"The what?"

"It's a novel—a very famous one, by Ayn Rand—"

"I don't read fiction," Jeff said. "I never have, except in school, when my teachers forced me."

"Of course not. You wouldn't." She looked crestfallen, then swiftly recovered. "Well, it was a movie, too—a grand old movie, with Gary Cooper and Patricia Neal—"

"Sorry." Jeff shook his head. "My father considered movies a waste of time."

Her chest rose and fell in a huff of disbelief that tightened the silk fabric across her luscious little breasts. "You should rent the video—or better yet, read the book. It's about an architect, a man named Howard Roark, who has so much integrity, so much passion, that he gives up everything, even the woman he loves, rather than compromise his work—"

"He sounds like an idealistic fool to me." Jeff was enjoying himself, watching the fire bursts of outrage that flared in her eyes.

"You're hopeless!" she snapped.

"And you're bewitching when you're angry. Has anyone ever told you that?"

"Oh, stop brushing me off as if I were a silly little twit without a brain in her head!" Her expressive hands stabbed the air like angry butterflies. "You're an impossible cynic, Jeff Parrish! Doesn't anything in your life truly matter to you?"

"Yes." Jeff had stopped smiling. "Ellen matters. She matters deeply. I suppose she's the only thing that really does."

"Well, at least you've got one priority in the right place," Kate muttered, setting down her glass and glancing around as if desperate to be rescued. "Oh, look, here comes the waiter with our dinners. I hope the food here is as good as you claim."

"How will you know? You'll only be eating the garnish."

Kate wrinkled her nose at him as the waiter whisked their plates onto the table. "It's a good thing we're not shooting for a serious relationship here," she said. "From what I've heard so far, I'd say you and I are about as compatible as a jellyfish and a porcupine."

"Dare I ask which of us is which?"

"Don't push me!" She picked up her fork and stabbed a chunk of romaine with a vehemence that made Jeff wince.

Taking his cue from her, he started on his own order of succulent blue crab drenched in garlic butter, mulling things over as he chewed. So far this evening, he'd managed to break Kate's precious souvenir, invade her privacy and needle her to the point of irritation. He had totally botched things from beginning to end, Jeff conceded.

So why was it he felt more alive, more sensually aware than he could remember feeling in years? Why was the wine an iridescent rainbow in his glass, each sip a miniature sunburst on his tongue? Why was Kate's little fox face glowing like a Madonna's in the soft, golden candlelight?

Why did he seem to sense her every heartbeat as if it were his own?

Jeff dropped his gaze to his plate, fighting a confusion that bordered on fear. The end of his marriage, followed so abruptly by Meredith's death, had left him emotionally frozen. Aside from his concern for Ellen, he had remained numb and unfeeling, mercifully anesthetized against the pain.

Now, he suddenly realized, he was beginning to feel— as he had never wanted to feel again.

Panic locked around Jeff's chest. It was as if he were standing on a precipice, gazing down into a sea of emotions he had sworn to leave behind for good. Anticipation...tenderness...vulnerability...regret. They were all there, waiting to pull him under. He wanted no part of them. He wanted to remain safe, to turn and walk swiftly away and never look back.

But even now, Jeff realized, it was too late to run. Seated across the table was a plucky little woman from a world he had never known. And whether he liked it or not, she was already weaving her way into his heart.

They had managed to get through the meal without sniping at each other—a minor miracle in itself, Kate reflected as she crumpled her napkin and placed it next to her half-emptied wineglass. After the opening volleys, the conversation had settled into a polite, if strained, dialogue about pottery throwing and glazing techniques, followed by a discussion of their daughters and how to oversee their time together.

She and Jeff had quickly agreed that the two little girls could not just be turned loose to wander on their own. But after that, negotiations had bogged down. They were still bogged down, and sinking deeper by the minute. Their fragile ceasefire, Kate sensed, was crumbling like a sand castle at high tide.

"I'm only asking for equal responsibility," she argued, brushing the last few croissant flakes off her skirt. "I know Flannery would be fine at your house, but I refuse to just dump her there and use your mother as a baby-sitting service."

Jeff stood up and strode around the table to help her with her chair. A perfect gentleman, Kate observed wryly. But then, wasn't that true of all summer men?

"I realize you don't want to impose," he said. "But believe me, Mother would never stand for your taking Ellen along on your Jo-Jo gigs."

"Your mother wouldn't stand for it? What about you?" Kate felt her temper flare like a forest fire racing up the trunk of a dry pine. "I'm not ashamed of what I do to make an honest living, and if it bothers you, you can—"

"Let's talk about it outside." His hand was hard against the small of her back as he guided her toward the door—as if he were afraid she might raise her voice and make a scene, Kate observed darkly.

"You didn't need to do that!" she muttered, twisting away from him as they stepped out onto the shadowed porch. "I wasn't about to start shouting in front of your fancy friends."

"Hush, Kate, it's not what you think." He had moved against the rail, where he stood gazing at her with brooding, unreadable eyes, the sea wind ruffling his moon-silvered hair. He looked like Heathcliff, she thought. Not the young, wild Heathcliff from the early pages of Emily Brontë's novel, but the mature, cynical hero, returning bitter and weary from the world. Heathcliff with a broken nose and a battered heart.

"Truce," he said, reaching out to take her arm. "Come on, let's go for a walk."

Softening, Kate allowed him to lead her down the zigzag boardwalk to the deserted beach. The tide was coming in, hissing up the long slope to crest in foamy ghost waves on the moon-paled sand. Darkening clouds fluttered like ragged chiffon streamers before the wind. A sandpiper skittered along the water's edge, then took flight with a lonely cry.

Kate's spike-heeled mules sank into the gritty sand with

each step. Impatient, she kicked them off, then slipped into the shadow of a dune to peel down her panty hose.

"No peeking!" she warned.

"What kind of rogue do you take me for?" Jeff's bravado was edged with a raw huskiness that puckered her skin to sensitive goose bumps. Tonight meant nothing, Kate reminded herself. Jeff Parrish might find it amusing to toy with her, and she wasn't above having a little fun of her own. But she could not afford to take his attentions seriously. The price was too high.

She would keep her wits about her, Kate resolved. She would remain icy cool, calm and detached. Above all, whatever happened, she would be the one in control.

"There, you can look." Kate wadded up her panty hose and stuffed them into her left shoe. "And now, Mr. Parrish, it's your turn."

"My turn?" His black eyebrows shot together above the bridge of his hunky nose. "And just what is it you're expecting me to do?"

"Take off your shoes, silly." She laughed, pretending to enjoy his confusion. "You said you wanted to go for a walk. Don't tell me you've never walked barefoot in the sand."

"Of course I have," he said, frowning. "I spent my boyhood summers right here in Misty Point, remember? But I'm not a boy anymore, and these shoes I'm wearing will do just fine."

"What's the matter?" she challenged him with a mocking grin. "Are you afraid of getting your feet wet?"

He hesitated. Then his breath rasped out in a sigh of defeat. He sank onto the bottom step of the boardwalk and began tugging at his shoelaces. Kate turned away to stroll along the edge of the surf, savoring the small victory while she could. From what she knew of Jefferson Parrish III, he was not likely to yield her many more of them.

Jeff forced himself to take his time, tugging off each sock, folding it flat and laying it inside its own shoe. His eyes remained on Kate where she stalked along the moonlit beach, the night breeze swirling her skirt around her incredible dancer's legs.

No, tonight had not been a good idea. Not any of it. Kate Valera was an accomplished witch, and she knew exactly what she was doing. The spell she was casting on him was one no healthy man could resist.

"Coming?" She glanced back over her shoulder, her curls fluttering like windblown petals across her cheeks. Cursing his own lack of judgment, Jeff scrambled to his feet, paused to roll up his trouser cuffs, then plunged after her.

The sand was wet and cool, its texture deliciously rough against his tingling bare soles. It felt wonderful until, sprinting to catch up with Kate, he stumbled over a half-buried chunk of driftwood, lost his balance, and crashed to his knees.

Laughing, she held out her hand to him. "Take it easy," she said as she playfully pulled him to his feet. "Don't get carried away."

Jeff kept her hand prisoner as he tried his weight on his stubbed toe. "You say this is supposed to be fun?" he muttered.

"Of course it is, if you let it." His heart jumped as her small, strong fingers invaded his palm, curling like warm tendrils into the empty spaces. "It's more than just fun," she said. "Relax. Get in touch with the earth and feel its power, that's what I tell the people in my yoga class."

"I'd rather get in touch with you." His warm grip tightened around hers as he used the leverage of her arm to yank her against his side. She stiffened warily.

"We do have some business to settle," she demurred.

"It's a beautiful night, Kate." Jeff waited for some kind of response from her. When it did not come, he loosened his clasp and sighed his acquiescence as her hand slipped away. "All right. The girls. Where did we leave off?"

"With my demanding equal responsibility," she said crisply. "I'll concede that it might not be the best idea to have Ellen along when I'm performing—for safety reasons, if nothing else. But I won't allow Flannery to simply be Ellen's little drop-off playmate."

"Kate—"

"I do have some free time," she said. "Maybe Ellen would like to make some pottery." Her enthusiasm faded as she took in his troubled expression. "What *is* it with you?" she asked, puzzled and hurt.

Jeff stared at a streak of reflected moonlight on the black water beyond the surf. He had done his best to push it out of his mind, but now the afternoon's scene with his mother returned in full clarity. *Mark my words, Jefferson, that Jo-Jo woman is trouble!* she had lectured him. *I'll tolerate her little girl if it makes Ellen happy, and I certainly can't stop you from slinking off to see her if you're foolish enough. But I won't stand for her influencing Ellen with her common ways! A child Ellen's age needs a proper role model, someone of her own social class!*

Kate was waiting for an answer, her lovely doe-like eyes glittering with wounded pride. What could he tell her? How could he explain the debt he owed his mother for taking on Ellen's care? How could he justify his own need for peace in the family—a peace that would shatter if he challenged her will?

He saw Kate's shoulders sag as she turned away. "Never

mind," she said. "It *is* your mother, isn't it? I should have known better than to ask."

"Blast it, Kate, it's not that simple," he said, despising himself. "Let's talk. We can work something out—"

"No, not another word. You may take me home. Now."

Jeff watched her, heartsick, as she took a step toward the boardwalk, then wheeled back to face him. "Flannery is to be on my doorstep first thing in the morning," she said coldly. "After that, we won't trouble you anymore. You can buy your daughter some other little wind-up friend to play with—a proper one who meets with your mother's approval."

As Jeff watched her turn away a second time, something snapped in him. Striding the distance between them, he seized her wrist. The momentum whipped her back against him, with her face a hand's breadth from his own.

Her pain-laced eyes gazed up at him, the pupils as wide and darkly mysterious as a cat's. Her trembling lips caught the gleam of moonlight, soft and moist and tempting.

Jeff knew his silence had hurt her. He wanted to explain himself, to tell her that he knew his mother's attitude wasn't right or fair. But talking wouldn't help, he knew. Kate wouldn't understand. She couldn't possibly understand. There was nothing he could say.

He could only kiss her.

His thumb caught the delicate curve of her jaw, gently bracing her as his mouth captured her soft, cool lips in a skillful play of flesh on flesh. Her lips were like cool silk, sweet with promise but little else. Even though she did not resist, Jeff could feel the tension between them as her will battled his, challenging him to make her respond.

Frustrated, he drew back. "Blast it, Kate, I'm only—"

"Only what?" She gazed at him with an innocence that made Jeff want to grind his teeth. "You kiss the way you design buildings," she said. "With flawless precision. No committee would fault you."

"Flawless precision. But no passion? Ha!" For all his bravado, Jeff found himself yearning for her—to clasp her in his arms again, to feel all that she was so stubbornly holding back from him.

His voice took on a tinge of menace. "All right, Ms. Smarty Pants. Suppose you give me a lesson or two."

She hesitated, a sudden wariness flashing in her eyes. Then, resolutely, she turned back toward the steps. "I think this dinner date, if that's what you want to call it, has lasted long enough," she said.

"Not so fast, lady." The words emerged as a husky growl as he reached out and caught her waist, snapping her against him. They stood quivering, breast to breast, hip to hip, their gazes hungrily locked. Jeff forced himself to hold back, aching for this woman, but knowing the next move would have to be hers, or the victory would be no victory at all.

It came when he least expected it, with a spontaneity that shook him to the soles of his feet. Kate's hand seized the back of his neck, pulling him down to her. Her mouth crushed itself like a flower against his lips.

Jeff caught her close, tenderness surging inside him like spring rain after a long, bleak winter. Need flamed up in him, warm and achingly sweet. Suddenly he could not get enough of her, her mouth on his, her lush little body in his arms.

"Kate..." he whispered. "You don't know...you can't know how much I've wanted this...."

"Hush." Her fingertip pressed his lips. "No words. Words are no good. They only hurt—they only lie—"

"All right, no words. No words, precious Kate." He kissed her cheeks, her temples, her eyelids, with the full fire of his awakened need. His tongue probed and penetrated, invading her mouth to lick and plunder a treasure trove of honey. She moaned, arching closer as his hands molded her softness to the hard planes of his chest and belly.

Heaven.

The night breeze sighed around them, fluttering her skirt against his legs. The rising surf washed up the beach to curl around their bare feet. At its first cold touch, Kate jumped back with a little cry.

"It's all right," Jeff muttered, pulling her gently back to him. "We don't have to stay here. We can go someplace else—to your house—"

"No!" She wrenched herself away and turned to face him, her eyes glittering with what could have been either rage or tears. "No—that's enough—"

Jeff's arms dropped to his side as he stared at her, dumbfounded. "Kate, I'm sorry," he muttered. "I thought—"

"Don't apologize." She backed away another step. "I *know* what you thought. Heaven knows, I didn't give you any reason to believe otherwise. But you're wrong, Jeff. I may be a romantic little fool, but I'm not—not a—tramp!" Her voice broke as she spat out the final word. Then she spun away, snatched up her sandals and bolted for the wooden staircase.

"Kate, if I've hurt you..." He stood as if rooted to the sand, watching her go. "Dammit, woman, what did I do?"

"Nothing." She paused, clinging to the rail. "It wasn't your fault. After the way I behaved, I can't blame you for thinking what any man would think. Now please take me home."

A cloud bank had drifted across the moon, darkening the night. Cursing under his breath, Jeff fumbled for the shoes he had left at the foot of the boardwalk. The devil of it was, Kate was wrong, he groused. She was a fine woman—he knew that, and he would never have pushed her farther than she wanted to go. When he'd suggested going to her house, he had only meant—

But what was the use? Even if he tried to explain, Kate would never listen, let alone believe him.

In the car, she sat with her hands clasped in her lap, responding in polite monosyllables to Jeff's lame stabs at conversation. Minutes passed, and he was beginning to seethe. Dammit, he didn't deserve this treatment, and he wasn't about to take it any longer. He was going to get through to this mule-headed little person if it took him all night.

Abruptly he turned the car onto a side road and pulled off into the mottled shadow of a big cypress tree. Kate flashed startled eyes at him as he switched off the ignition and unfastened his seat belt. "Don't worry, I'm not going to touch you," he said. "But this is honesty time. Once and for all, Kate Valera, I intend to find out what's—"

He broke off, silently cursing himself as the moon silvered a single gleaming tear on her cheek. Suddenly all he wanted to do was gather her in his arms, dry her tears and protect her from the whole hurtful world.

Protect her from men like himself.

"Tonight was a mistake," she whispered. "I was playing with fire, and I thought I could handle it. I was wrong."

Jeff kept his distance, knowing it was essential to keeping her trust. "I would never hurt you, Kate," he said softly.

"I'm afraid that's a chance I can't afford to take." She rippled an agitated hand through her windblown curls. "You're a very compelling man, Jeff, and I'll admit you had me going back there. But it's no good. I'm getting too old and fragile to pick up all the pieces when summer ends and you walk away. And you *will* walk away. Don't even try to deny it."

Jeff rolled down the window, taking his time, knowing he could not insult her with a lie. The chirp of crickets blended with the distant murmur of the waves. "We have two little girls who want to be friends," he said. "Couldn't you and I be friends, too?"

"I...truly don't know." Her breath eased out in a ragged sigh. "Right now my mind is spinning like a whirligig. It must be the wine. I think you'd better get me home."

"Will you think about it?" he persisted, dismayed at the thought that he might not see her again. "Tomorrow, maybe, when you're feeling better?"

"In the cold, gray light of dawn?" She managed a frayed laugh. "We'll see."

"I like you, Kate." He switched on the ignition and swung the car back onto the road. "Whatever else you choose to believe about my motives, believe that."

"I'll try to keep it in mind." She tugged her rumpled skirt over her enticingly bare knees as Jeff tried to focus his attention on his driving. His emotions, he realized, were pumping like the pistons of a runaway steam locomotive. This was insane, he told himself. If he let this woman get under his skin, he had no more sense than a hormone-driven nineteen-year-old.

It was with mixed feelings that he pulled into her driveway and strode around to let her out of the car. Put an end to this hopeless encounter—that would be a mercy to them both, Jeff lectured himself as he battled the urge to sweep her into his arms one last time. Kate Valera was a delectable package from her untamed auburn curls to the tips of her little shell pink toes, and the chemistry that had blazed between them on the beach was still setting off miniature rocket bursts in his veins. But the last thing Kate needed was an embittered cynic who was only looking for a summer diversion. And the last thing *he* needed was open warfare with his mother.

"I, uh, hope you'll understand if I don't invite you in," she said as they reached the porch.

The remark struck Jeff as so ludicrous that he could not hold back a chuckle. It burst out of him half-muffled, like air escaping from a stretched balloon. Kate glanced up at him, her eyes startled and uncertain.

"What's the matter now?" she asked.

"Nothing," Jeff said, feeling the tension lift a little. "You're all right, Kate Valera."

"And what brought on this change of heart?"

"No change. I always thought you were all right. More than all right. You're a gutsy, intelligent, very sexy lady." Facing her, he held out his right hand. "Friends?"

The breath quivered out of her in a little sigh. "All right. Friends. But don't expect anything more. I'm not up to it, Jeff. I mean that."

"You've got a deal." He shook her hand, savoring the feel of her strong, cool fingers for as long as she would allow it. He ached to gather her into his arms again, to hold her close and warm her mouth to flame with his kisses. But he knew better than to try. Besides, she was already backing away from him, fumbling for her key in the tiny black satin bag she'd brought along in the car.

"Good night, Kate," he said, feigning a hard-edged smile. "Thank you for a most memorable evening."

"And thank you for...dinner." She had found her key and was turning it in the lock. Suddenly she hesitated. "Wait here," she ordered him. "There's something I want to give you."

Before Jeff could say another word, she had flashed into the house. He prowled the shadowy porch as the seconds ticked past, fighting the temptation to follow her as a lamp flickered on in the living room. His hands fidgeted with his car keys.

A minute or two later she reappeared with something in her hand. "A present," she whispered. "Don't look at it until you get home." She thrust the object into the pocket of his jacket. It felt thick and solid—a paperback book, he realized, half intrigued, half-skeptical. Maybe the lady was into some kind of New Age self-help program or bizarre Eastern philosophy, and she wanted to share it with him. Sure. That was all he needed.

But then, what difference did it make? Jeff reminded himself. If the book contained more pieces of the Kate Valera puzzle, he knew he would read every word of it.

After a mercifully swift good-night, he found himself in the car, headed for his own house. He took deep breaths and tried to relax, but fragments of the evening kept floating to the surface of his mind. Kate, gazing at him over her wineglass with those unsettling aquamarine eyes. Kate in his arms, warm, fragrant and trembling, fitting against his body as if she had been molded there. Kate angry and proud, her head held high, her small hands balled into indignant fists.

Kate.

Blast the woman!

Jeff's muscles ached with nervous tension, and he knew this would be no night for easy sleep. Maybe it was a good thing Kate had given him something to read.

Something. But what?

Overcome by sudden curiosity, he pulled the car off the road and clicked on the dome light. She had told him not to look at the book until he got home, but he was tired and running out of patience. Besides, he rationalized, the family cottage was no more than a few minutes away.

Unfastening his seat belt, Jeff worked the thick volume out of his pocket, held it up to the light and uttered a half-bemused groan.

Clutched in his hand was a dog-eared paperback copy of *The Fountainhead.*

Kate stood slumped against the inside door frame, staring into the silent darkness of the living room. Her head ached, her feet hurt, and her stomach felt as if she'd just swallowed a school of live guppies.

Her cheeks burned hot with humiliation as her mind ticked mercilessly through the past couple of hours. Her idiotic conversation. Her angry defensiveness. Her soul-melting surrender to the raw power of Jeff Parrish's kiss.

How on earth had she managed to make such a complete fool of herself?

And what had possessed her to give Jeff the book? By now, he was probably laughing himself silly at her expense. She should have held back her opinions, Kate lectured herself. She should have fluttered her eyelashes and played dumb, helpless and worshipful—that was probably what he expected of a woman.

But what difference should it make? She certainly had no designs on Mr. Jefferson Parrish III, so why should it matter what he or his mother thought of her?

Why should it matter what anyone thought? she reminded herself angrily. She was her own person. She lived by her own standards, made her own choices and answered to no one but herself. What was more, she liked it that way!

Forcing herself to move, she crossed the living room and strode down the hall. Without Flannery, the house was silent and lonely. She would go to bed now and get a good night's rest, Kate resolved. Then she would get up early and spend the morning in her pottery studio. When Jeff came to drop Flannery off, she would be conveniently busy—too busy to spend any time with him.

It was a cool and logical plan. But when she stepped into her own bedroom, the wave of emotion that swept over her was so overpowering that she could hardly stand. There was no use evading the truth any longer. For the first time in years, she had met a man she could love. A man she could adore, coddle, worship, tease and cherish. And he was far beyond her reach. The whole situation was one miserable black joke.

Overcome by despair, Kate flung herself headlong onto the cushions piled at the head of her bed—only to have her anguished sob interrupted by a startled feline yowl.

Spitting like grease on a red-hot stove, Mehitabel exploded from among the cushions, leapt straight into the air and rocketed out of the room.

For an instant Kate sat wild-eyed and quivering in the darkness. As she realized what had happened, she began to giggle, then to laugh. Helpless peals of hilarity shook her body. She laughed until her sides ached and the tears ran down her cheeks.

Yes, it had to be the wine. She should never have allowed herself to take so much as a sip.

Little by little the giggles subsided and her mind began to clear. At least she knew that Flannery hadn't smuggled the cat to Ellen's house in her backpack, as she'd feared earlier.

But if Mehitabel was here, what had been in Flannery's pack? Jeff had mentioned it was heavy—

Puzzled and concerned, Kate got up and hurried across the hall to her daughter's bedroom.

A flip of the light switch revealed nothing unusual in the milieu of Flannery's creative clutter. Her clothes lay wherever she had stepped out of them. Notepads, paper and markers were strewn on the rug. The shelves above her bed—

Yes, Kate realized with a sinking sensation in the pit of her stomach, all Flannery's favorite books were missing. *The Brothers Grimm; Hans Christian Andersen: The Wizard of Oz; The Chronicles of Narnia.* Even Kate's own loveworn childhood volume of Rose Fyleman's fairy poems was gone.

Kate groaned out loud as the truth sank home. Flannery had taken the books to Ellen's house and, unless caught by Jeff's mother, had spent the evening filling her little friend's head with forbidden fantasies.

Either way, there would be the devil to pay.

Chapter Six

Kate was working at her pottery wheel when Jeff walked into the studio. Morning sunlight from the east window glinted on his damply curling hair. His steel gray eyes were shadowed and bloodshot, as if he'd had trouble sleeping.

Well, that was tough, Kate reminded herself. She hadn't exactly slept like a baby herself.

Struggling to blur the memory of last night's kiss, she kicked the wheel faster and fixed her attention on the tall pot she was throwing. It was no use. The first sight of him had completely undone her concentration. Guided by her unsteady hands, the pot lost its center and began to wobble. Seconds later it collapsed into a lopsided mass of crumpled, wet clay.

"Did I do that?" he asked only half-apologetically.

"It happens." Kate shrugged, acutely conscious of his gaze taking in her clay-spattered face, hands, hair and smock. She wondered if he'd discovered her daughter's cache of forbidden stories. Maybe she should bring the matter up herself. "So where's Flannery?" she asked.

"The girls are in the living room with your cat. They're fine." She sensed an expectant seething in him, a mustering of dark emotions, as if he were working himself up to read her the riot act.

Kate braced herself for the storm, ready to admit her own failing in the matter. For all her decent intentions, she had never really gotten around to telling Flannery that fairy tales were a no-no for her new friend—maybe because she'd been so appalled by the idea herself. Denying a child's fantasy was barbaric and cruel. If Jeff Parrish pressed her hard enough, she would tell him exactly that.

"Is something wrong?" she demanded when he did not speak up right away.

His gray eyes blackened like thunderclouds. "You knew exactly what you were doing last night, didn't you?"

"I don't know what you're talking about," Kate protested, opting for the coward's way out.

"The devil you don't. That book. That blasted hunk of pulp you shoved into my pocket."

"*The Fountainhead?*" She blinked at him, thrown off balance by the unexpected shift. Apparently he hadn't discovered Flannery's storybooks after all. It was her own silly, impulsive gesture that had upset him.

"Look at me!" he snapped. "I didn't sleep at all last night! I spent the whole time reading, and this morning I'm a snarling, baggy-eyed wreck!"

Kate couldn't help it. A corner of her mouth twitched; then she giggled.

Jeff shot her a glare, then plunged ahead. "That's not the worst of it," he said. "After I'd read the part of the story where Roark dynamites his own housing project rather than see his design spoiled by bureaucrats, I tossed the book aside, marched up to my studio, and looked at my plans for the hospital wing—really looked at them for what they were—a mediocre hodge-podge designed to please a committee!''

Kate was no longer laughing. Her hands rested quietly on the clay as she saw the turmoil in him and realized it was, in part, her doing.

She had given Jeff the book as a tease, a gentle shakeup for his all-too-rigid outlook. Never, in her wildest dreams, had she imagined what it would do to him.

''I tore the plans up,'' he said. ''I threw them in the trash and started over. The new design isn't fully worked out yet, but it's going to be different from anything I've ever done. Different—and better.''

Relief swept over Kate like sunlight breaking through a cloud. ''That's wonderful, Jeff!'' she exclaimed. ''I'm so happy—so glad—''

''Don't be. I know that hospital board. When they see the new plans, they'll nail my hide to the wall. I'll end up designing taco franchises in Snowflake, Arizona.''

''Don't!'' Concerned now, Kate had swung off her bench and was moving toward him, navigating through the clutter of vats, shelves and boxes. ''Don't do this to yourself. You're writing your own bad script before it happens—''

''Writing my own script? Is that one of those platitudes you spoon-feed your yoga students?'' Jeff's eyes glinted dangerously. ''You should have left well enough alone, Kate. You should have left that damned book on the shelf where it belongs. And you should have left me in that merciful, anesthetized stupor where you found me!''

His hand darted out and caught her wrist. A canister of cadmium glaze crashed to the floor as he spun her hard against him.

Quivering, Kate forced herself to meet the tempered steel in his eyes. ''I thought we were friends,'' she declared, refusing to be intimidated.

"So did I."

He hesitated for the space of a heartbeat. Then his arms encircled her waist, and his lips closed on hers with a tender fury that melted her mouth to his. Kate willed herself to struggle, but the resistance was all in her mind. Her body was already responding like wax to a blowtorch. Desire flashed through her as her arms went around him. Shooting stars danced pirouettes in her head. She clung to Jeff Parrish as if he were the only solid object in a Tilt-A-Whirl universe that was spinning faster and faster.

"This...wasn't the kind of friendship I had in mind...." she stammered as their moist, swollen mouths finally broke apart.

"Neither did I." A hard recklessness glittered in his eyes as Kate struggled to retrieve the scattered fragments of her common sense.

"Jeff, this is insane!" she whispered. "You—me—everything about this is wrong. There's no possible future in it! We can't just—"

"Listen to me, Kate." His hands clasped her shoulders, holding her fast. His eyes were a magnet to her gaze, savage, tender and compelling. "I don't know where this wild ride is going to lead, and I'd be a hypocritical fool to promise you anything at the end of it. I only know that you make me feel alive for the first time in years, and whatever's out there for us, I don't want to miss it."

Kate strained against his hands, elation mingling with despair. At least he had been honest with her. There'd been no platitudes. No promises. No guarantees of anything except here and now.

One day, Kate knew, Jeff Parrish would break her heart.

But she did not have the strength to walk away from him now.

"Let go of my arms," she whispered.

His hands released her and dropped abruptly to his sides. She saw the icy cynicism slide back into his eyes, then saw it melt like morning frost as she reached for him. Her heart lifted like a bird as he caught her close once more in an embrace that was as bittersweet as it was passionate.

She raised her face for his kiss. That was when the duet of giggles reached her ears. She glanced past Jeff to see Flannery and Ellen standing in the studio doorway, convulsed with mischievous titters.

"You little monkeys!" Kate exclaimed, forcing a nervous laugh as she and Jeff broke awkwardly apart. "How long have you been standing there?"

"Long enough." Flannery was grinning like Lewis Carroll's Cheshire Cat.

"Does this mean you're going to get married?" Ellen piped, her soft eyes dancing.

"It most certainly does not!" Kate's cheeks had grown uncomfortably warm. Jeff's face, she noticed, was the hue of a ripe raspberry beneath his suntan.

"It just means that we—uh—like each other, that's all," he said, wiggling his shoulders in an odd little shrug that touched off a warning flicker in Kate's heart.

"Well, it looks to me as if you like each other a lot," said Flannery. "*I've* certainly never kissed anybody that way!"

Kate bit back the urge to throttle her precious daughter. "Hey," she said, "I think I've got some leftover blueberry bran muffins and juice in the kitchen. Would anybody like breakfast?"

"Floss fixed us ham and eggs this morning," Flannery said. "I've never had ham before. It was *good!* Why don't you ever fix it?"

Kate rolled her eyes toward the ceiling as Jeff did a fair job of suppressing a smile. "We'll pass on breakfast," he said, but we want to invite you to a beach picnic this afternoon if you can make it. Ellen and Flannery cooked up the idea, and I couldn't see any reason to try and talk them out of it. I'll be spending most of the day on the new hospital wing plans, but I should be ready for a break about three or so. We can grab some sandwiches at the deli—don't worry, I'll make sure yours is vegetarian.''

''Sorry, but you'll have to go without me.'' Kate's reply blended disappointment with relief. Things were happening too fast. She needed time to sort things out, time to get her bearings before flinging herself headlong into this scary new involvement. ''I'll be doing Jo-Jo at Shop 'n' Save till three-thirty, and then I've got a two-year-old birthday party. But don't let that spoil your plans. Flannery's welcome to go along if you don't mind picking her up at the shopping center.''

''Oh, but it wouldn't be any fun without you.'' Ellen had scampered over to tug at Kate's hand with heart-melting sweetness. ''We can wait till tomorrow, or even the next day for our picnic, can't we, Daddy?''

''That certainly suits me.'' Jeff's eyes flickered warmly from Kate to his daughter and back again. ''How's tomorrow?''

Kate sighed. ''Jo-Jo again—a nursery school in Kitty Hawk. By the time I drive over there and back...'' She paused, dismayed by the sight of three long faces. ''But I have the next day free. How's that?''

''Fine!'' three voices chimed in unison, and Kate suddenly felt as if the jaws of a trap were closing around her. There was so much potential for hurt here—for the girls, for herself, even for Jeff. She would be wise to speak up now, to put a stop to this whole ill-fated adventure.

But whatever wisdom she might possess was dimmed by the glow in two pairs of little-girl eyes, and by the presence of a man who held her heart prisoner in the palm of his warm, strong hand.

Suddenly she felt shaky all over.

She ought to come clean about Flannery's books right now, Kate told herself. Get it out in the open before it had time to fester like an infected splinter—that would be the smart thing to do. But when she looked at the happy faces around her, the words would not come.

"Goodness, look at the time!" she sputtered, giving way to panic. "I—I'm afraid you'll have to excuse me. I need to shower off this clay and be at Shop 'n' Save in full costume and makeup by ten."

"That sounds like our cue, honey." Jeff caught Ellen's shoulder and scooped her toward him. "Let's hit the road and let Jo-Jo here start her day. It was nice having you with us, Miss Flannery Valera, author." He shook the grinning child's hand. "Please come back anytime."

His eyes met Kate's above the heads of their daughters, the contact as intimate as a caress. Waves of tender need shimmered through her body. She was out of her depth here, Kate realized, and she was sinking fast.

"I'll call you," his lips whispered, and she could only nod as he smiled and turned away. Poor Kate. Poor, dumb, hooked fish.

Flannery stood on the porch, waving as the gray BMW pulled out of the drive. Then she pranced back into the living room, a happy grin on her sharp, freckled face.

"I knew it!" she said. "I knew you liked him! And he likes you, too! Wow, what a kiss!"

"Don't read too much into that kiss." Kate tugged at the buttons of her clay-spattered smock with fingers that felt like squiggly molded Jell-O. "Liking somebody is one thing. Planning a life together is quite another."

"But you'd make such a great couple—and then Ellen

and I could be sisters! Ellen wants that, too. She told me—''

"Ellen and her father are summer people," Kate said, aching for her daughter. "When the season ends, they'll be going back to Raleigh. You've got to be prepared for that, Flannery. Otherwise, it's going to hurt you."

"But it isn't right!" Flannery argued. "If I were writing a story about this, I'd give it a happy ending, with all of us a family."

"I'm afraid this isn't a story, sweetheart. This is real life."

"Well I think real life stinks!" Flannery punched a sofa cushion, startling Mehitabel into slinking retreat. "All I ever wanted was a dad, like other kids have. Why did my father have to die before I ever even saw him?"

"Because life is like that." Kate sat down and gathered her daughter close. "Sometimes life can be mean and cruel and take away what you love most. Other times—well, it's as if life turns around and gives you a beautiful present all wrapped up in a silver ribbon—a present so fantastic that you can hardly believe you're not dreaming." She kissed Flannery's wild orange curls. "You're my present, little mermaid. And because of you, I can't help believing that life's been more than fair with me."

Flannery squirmed restlessly. "Does that mean you'll buy me a chocolate yogurt shake and some fries on the way to Shop 'n' Save?"

Kate laughed in spite of her worries. "All right, *if* there's time. Come on, you little opportunist, let's get washed and changed before the whole morning gets away from us!"

Jeff rubbed one forearm across his sweat-blurred eyes. The overhead fan in his studio had developed a nerve-grinding squeak, but the day was too hot to switch it off.

If he ever spent another summer here, he swore, he'd pay through the nose to install central air-conditioning.

A glance at his watch revealed that it was almost four in the afternoon. He'd been working on the new plans for so long that time had lost its meaning. But the design was still the best thing he'd ever done. Daring, innovative and highly functional, it blended the hospital's existing structure with the sweeping, modern lines of the new wing. Selling his plan to the conservative hospital board wouldn't be easy—he could only hope his own excitement would carry the day. Otherwise, he resolved, they could blasted well find themselves another architect—at least that's what Howard Roark would have said.

Pausing to stretch his cramped shoulders, he reached for his iced tea glass and swigged the melting ice at the bottom. What had gotten into him, anyway? He felt as if he had a fire blazing through his veins—as if every nerve in his body was tingling with awareness. The feeling was as painful as it was exhilarating.

Passion, Kate had called it.

A tender smile played about Jeff's lips. His fingertips fondled the faceted contours of the glass as he remembered Kate clasped tight against him, fiery and vulnerable, her kiss awakening him to a whole magical world. Kate laughing. Kate crying. Kate cradling her bewitching elf-child in her arms.

Kate, who had turned his whole world upside down and given it a much-needed shaking.

Was he falling in love with her?

The idea was too crazy to even consider, Jeff lectured himself. They were from different worlds, he and Kate. They had different goals, different values. Meshing their two life-styles would be like—

"Jefferson!" His mother's voice, shrill with agitation,

shattered his train of thought. He braced himself, resolving to be patient as her heavy tread echoed along the upstairs hallway, marching closer.

"Jefferson, have you seen what that child of yours is doing?" She appeared in the doorway, arms akimbo, one hand clutching a pad of Ellen's drawing paper. "I could have told you things would come to this!" she exclaimed, thrusting it under his nose. "Now what are we going to do?"

Jeff took the sketchbook, opened its cover and began to slowly turn the pages. The first few sketches he had seen before—a drawing of the house, two pictures of seashells and a sailboat in the cove. Next there was a newer picture of a sleeping cat that bore a skillful likeness to Mehitabel. Ellen had inherited his own artistic talent and then some, Jeff conceded with a little stab of pride. Maybe one day she would follow her father into architecture.

Then he turned the page.

"See?" his mother hissed as he stared in shocked silence. "What did I tell you?"

The paper was peopled with exquisitely drawn little fairies. Fairies hovering. Fairies preening. Fairies dancing and bowing or resting on ruffled flower petals.

"It's that Jo-Jo woman's doing!" Jeff's mother snapped.

"Her name is Kate, Mother." He hadn't meant to sound irritable, but he did. Kate knew how he felt about exposing Ellen to fantasy. The least she could have done was respect his wishes and make sure her daughter did the same.

"I knew it," his mother huffed. "We should never have allowed that horrid child to spend the night here."

"Flannery's not a horrid child," he argued, defending her in spite of his dismay. "She's just a bright little girl with a very active imagination. I'm sure she meant no harm."

"Well, you certainly can't say the same thing for her mother! The woman's a fortune hunter, Jefferson. She's out to entrap you, and she's certainly not above—"

"That's enough, Mother," Jeff said quietly. "Now, just relax while I go and talk to Ellen. I'm sure we can get to the bottom of this situation."

"I already know what's at the bottom of it!" Jeff's mother sank into a leather armchair and fanned her damp chest with an old issue of *Architectural Digest*. "Mark my words, Jefferson, if you've got the sense you were born with, you'll send those two redheaded troublemakers packing before your daughter suffers permanent harm!"

Not trusting himself to answer, Jeff turned and strode out of the studio. His emotions churned as he walked downstairs to the dining room where Ellen sat with her art supplies spread out on one end of the long table.

"Hi, Daddy." Her expression was as innocent as a puppy's. "Oh, good, you brought my drawing pad back. I was afraid when Grandma took it—"

"Honey, we've got to talk." Jeff pulled out a chair, sat down across from her and opened the sketch pad to the page with the fairies.

"Uh, okay. What about?" Her eyes were luminous silver pools. This was not going to be easy.

"For starters, why don't you tell me about this picture?" he said, handing her the pad.

"These are fairies!" She leaned toward him, her voice hushed with wonder. "They all live in a magic garden, and this one with the crown, she's the fairy queen. She has a magic wand, and she uses it to make…" The words faded as she took in his pained expression.

"You don't like it, do you?" she whispered.

"It's a very nice drawing," Jeff hedged. "The only trouble is, fairies aren't real."

"How do you know that, Daddy?"

"Because it's true. Everybody knows it is."

"Not everybody," Ellen insisted. "If you believe in fairies—*really* believe—they can be as real as we are. That's what Flannery says."

Jeff sighed, feeling strangely old and tired. "So it's Flannery who's been filling your head with this nonsense."

"But it *isn't* nonsense! It's important! When people stop believing in fairies, all the fairies will die! It says so in one of Flannery's books!"

Jeff suppressed a groan. "Ellen," he said, straining for patience, "what have I always told you about truth?"

"That truth is the key to every door in this world—but, Daddy, how do we know what truth is?"

"Truth is what's real, Ellen. It's what we can see and hear and touch. Fairies aren't real. Neither are mermaids."

She gazed at him as if he were a backward child. "Remember that book you gave me last year? The one about gravity?"

"Uh-huh." Jeff sensed a trap sliding open beneath him.

"Can you see gravity? Can you hear it? Can you touch it?"

"Blast it, Ellen—"

"Listen to me, Daddy." Her hand on his arm was as soft and light as a kitten's paw. "If I can believe in mermaids and fairies, I can believe in Mommy. I know her body is in the ground, but I can believe that part of her is someplace beautiful, and that she still loves me."

"Ellen—" Jeff blinked to clear his blurring vision.

"Don't you see?" she said, patting his wrist. "I *want* to believe. Believing is fun, and it makes me happy."

Jeff's shoulders sagged in the face of his daughter's earnestness. The psychiatrist had insisted that she be forced to deal with reality, but Ellen, with Flannery's help, had created her own fantasy world and taken refuge there.

Would that world heal her or harm her? Jeff had no way of knowing, but he was deeply worried.

"Daddy, are you all right?" Ellen tugged at his sleeve. "I'm sorry. I didn't mean to make you feel bad."

"I'm fine, honey." Jeff exhaled sharply, groping for a way to express his concern without crushing her fragile spirit. He was still struggling with the words when the phone rang. Excusing himself, he caught it in the living room.

"Jeff?" Kate's husky little voice sent a freshet of warmth surging through his body. He had every reason to be furious with her, he reminded himself. But even now, his anger was washing away in a flood of anticipation.

"Hi, what's up?" he asked, trying to sound casual.

There was a long silence on the line. Then the words spilled out like water gushing through a broken dike. "I'm so sorry to bother you—I know you must be working—but I just got home, and I..." She paused, and Jeff heard her swallow hard. "There's something that's been chewing on my conscience all day, and I'm afraid I can't let it go any longer."

Her voice was raw with strain. Suddenly he was concerned for her. "Look, how bad can it be?" he joked lamely. "Whatever you've done, I forgive you. All right?"

"Wait till you hear," she said. "Remember your comment about Flannery's heavy backpack? She wasn't smuggling the cat in it. She was smuggling her books—all those fairy tales you think are so awful—"

Jeff stifled a groan. "Kate, I'm not blaming you—"

"But that's just it—you should. You see, I never told Flannery the books were forbidden. Oh, I meant to, but every time I tried, the words created such a nasty taste in my mouth that I could never bring myself to say them.''

Jeff twisted the phone cord in his fingers, torn between an angry retort and the desire not to hurt her. ''Seeing the damage has already been done,'' he said, ''there's no point in—''

''No, let me finish,'' she interrupted. ''I can't truly say I'm sorry because I'm not. I just didn't want you blaming Flannery for something she did in complete innocence.''

''Look, Kate, it's not a question of blame. It's a question of where we take it from here.'' Jeff glimpsed Ellen in the doorway, watching him with somber gray eyes.

''Maybe we should cancel our beach picnic,'' Kate said. ''Maybe we should cancel…everything. Flannery will be hurt, but she'll get over it. So will Ellen.''

Jeff felt something slipping away from him, and suddenly he knew he could not let it go. ''I don't want to disappoint the girls,'' he said. ''No, that's not all of it—I don't want to disappoint *me*.''

''But we know where this is going—it's going nowhere.''

''We don't know that, Kate. At this point, we don't know anything.''

Her sigh crackled static on the line. ''All right. We've got a couple of days to let things settle. Then we can try to enjoy a nice, civilized picnic. After that—''

''After that we'll take this one step at a time. Agreed?''

She was silent for no more than a heartbeat, but Jeff felt as if eternity were passing before him.

''Agreed—for now,'' she said at last. ''Goodbye, Jeff.''

He cradled the receiver in his palm for a moment after she hung up, reluctant to let her go. Ellen had wandered into the living room. As Jeff forced himself to replace the phone on its hook, she sank onto an old leather ottoman, where she sat gazing at him expectantly.

"Well, is Kate going to be my new mother or not?" she asked.

Jeff struggled to convert a choking sound into a laugh. "Kate and I barely know each other, honey. What ever gave you that idea?"

"I saw you kissing. People don't do that unless they love each other. They kiss and then they get married."

Jeff sagged into a chair, at a loss for words.

"Oh, it's okay with me," Ellen added quickly. "I like Kate. I think having a clown for a mother would be very nice. And having Flannery for a sister would be even nicer."

"Well, don't get your hopes up," Jeff said. "I...uh, don't think Kate is interested in marrying me."

"Oh, but she is!" Ellen's eyes sparkled. "Just ask Flannery!"

"Flannery who?" Jeff bantered. "Oh, you mean the Flannery who makes up stories about fairies and mermaids! *That* Flannery says her mother wants to marry me!"

Ellen giggled. "Daddy, you're impossible!"

"No, just highly improbable." Jeff reached out and playfully nudged her cheek. "How about a game of checkers?"

"You promised to teach me chess when I turned nine."

"Okay. But no more mermaids or fairies for the rest of the day. And no more talk about my marrying anybody. Deal?"

"Deal. I'll get the chess set."

As Ellen skipped to the game cupboard, Jeff sank back into the chair and stared up at the whirling blades of the ceiling fan. His thoughts seemed to be spinning with it.

Marry Kate?

The whole idea was a joke. They were nothing alike, he

and feisty little Kate Valera. Their life together would be one constant battle—oh, they would never run out of things to fight about. They could fight about his rich friends and bourgeois life-style. They could fight about his mother. They could fight about how to raise their children. And if those issues got old, they could even fight about what to put on the damned dinner table.

At least their lives would never be dull.

Or lonely.

"Daddy, I've got the chessboard and the pieces. Come on, let's play!" Ellen called from the dining room.

Jeff pulled himself out of the chair. He had always enjoyed chess, and had looked forward to teaching Ellen how to play. But today he knew it would take all his effort to keep his mind on the game.

Did Kate play chess? He wouldn't bet on it, Jeff decided. From what he knew of the woman, he couldn't imagine her liking anything that involved sitting still and thinking. She was like a bright little hummingbird, always moving, flitting, gesturing, leaving iridescent rainbow flashes where she passed...

Marry Kate Valera? The whole notion was preposterous!

So why had his heart jumped when Ellen mentioned the idea?

"Daddy?" Ellen's silver bell voice sang out from the dining room.

"Coming." Jeff double-timed his step. He couldn't afford to dwell on Kate too much, he warned himself. They had a friendship, that was all. An interesting friendship. A lively, warm friendship.

Warm.

Like a blazing forest fire.

For two days Kate had been searching desperately for an excuse to miss the picnic. She had not found one. Now here she and Flannery were, dressed in their swimsuits and cover-ups, their fair skins slicked with sunscreen, their beach hamper crammed with towels, lotion, a pail and shovel, a battered pair of binoculars and a carefully wrapped basket of homemade mango tarts.

Here they were, waiting for Jeff and Ellen to arrive.

"Now remember, no running off," she cautioned her daughter for the third time that day. "You and Ellen are to stay within sight of us at all times. And no going into deep water. Nothing above your shoulders. Understand?"

"Understand." Flannery bounded to the window. "Here they are! Oh, goody! They brought Ellen's grandma!"

"What? Oh, no!" Panic shot through Kate as she struggled to hide her dismay. "Why didn't they tell me she was—"

"Gotcha, Mom!" Flannery giggled like a carrot-topped maniac, skipped to the front door and flung it open. "Hey," she shouted. "My mom says to put your stuff in the Jeep! That way we won't get sand in your nice car!"

Kate heard Jeff saying something in response, followed by the expensively muted click of the trunk opening. When she mustered the courage to look out the window she saw Jeff, Flannery and Ellen hauling beach gear from the BMW to the Jeep. There was no sign of the redoubtable Mrs. Parrish. That Flannery!

Kate forced her face into a friendly smile. "Hi!" she chirped, striding out onto the porch with the hamper. "Nice day for a picnic, isn't it?"

Jeff turned around and grinned at her. He was meltingly handsome in boxer trunks and a matching denim beach jacket that set off his golden bronze skin. Through the jacket's open front Kate glimpsed a strip of rock-hard belly and crisp, black chest hair. He looked so delicious that she could have licked him like an ice cream cone.

As his eyes appraised her warmly, she glanced down and noticed that the sunless tanning lotion she'd applied so carefully last night had left an orange streak down her left leg. Its color clashed hideously with the pale pink polish on her toenails. She considered dashing inside to throw on long pants, but it was too late.

"You look terrific," Jeff said.

"Sure." She locked the door and strode toward the Jeep. Maybe she could get the kids to bury her in sand from the neck down. Or better yet, she could swim out to the Gulf Stream and get nibbled by hungry sharks. Anything would be less painful than spending the afternoon tantalizing herself with a man she could never have.

"I'll drive," she said, swinging into the Jeep. "Into the back, ladies, and fasten your seat belts. Yours, too, Mr. Parrish."

"I take it you've figured out where we're going." The note of wry amusement in Jeff's voice raked across her already raw nerves.

"There's a little inlet a half mile off the ferry road," she said, grinding the gears as she shifted the Jeep into reverse. "It's sheltered from the waves, with a long slope of shallow water. I thought it would be nice and safe for the girls."

"Good thinking." He settled back in his seat, wind ruffling his thick silver hair as the Jeep rolled down the highway. "I stopped at Fenster's for sandwiches and drinks," he said. "I hope you like sprouts and avocado on wheat."

"That's fine." Kate glanced back to confirm that the girls weren't listening. "And I suppose you got ham and cheese for Flannery."

"I did—but only at Flannery's request."

"Ham in exchange for fairy tales. I'd say that trade puts us just about even, Mr. Parrish."

His breath caught as if someone had poked him sharply in the stomach. Then he laughed, a sound so deep and warm that Kate knew she would hear it forever in her dreams.

"You're all right, Kate Valera," he said.

"Are you sure?" She shot him a sidelong glance and caught him in the midst of a heart-shattering smile.

"You're a breath of fresh air," he said. "No—that's a cliché. What you really are is a miniature cyclone, blowing into my life, stirring everything into tumult and confusion—"

"Oh, please!" The tires spat gravel as she swung the Jeep off the main highway, onto the ferry road. "What have I done to deserve such praise?"

"More than you know. You've made me angry. You've made me laugh. You've damn near made me cry—"

"And that's *good?*"

His hand reached for hers where it rested on the gearshift knob. For Kate, the brief pressure of his fingers was sweet torture. "It's good," he said.

She swung the vehicle onto a narrow, graveled side road that wound through the brush to disappear among the dunes. "I wish you wouldn't say that," she said softly. "It scares me. You can't imagine how much it scares me."

"Why, Kate?"

"Don't."

"Why does it scare you to hear the truth?"

"Because it isn't the truth—not the whole truth, at least. You're having fun with me, that's all."

He grinned engagingly. "Well, you're half-right. I *am* having fun with you. But that isn't all. Not by any means."

"I said, don't."

"Tell me what you're really afraid of, Kate." His huskily voiced demand sent a thrill through her body, touching off a clamor of alarms. Suddenly she felt as if she were being pulled into a whirlpool. Panic-stricken, she knew she had to break free.

"Look, girls!" she sang out, pointing to a speck in the hot blue sky. "Isn't that a long-billed curlew? Flannery—hurry, grab the binoculars and take a look!"

Relief washed over her as the girls responded, laughing and rummaging through the beach hamper till they came up with the binoculars.

"Do you see it?" Kate egged them on. "There—just ahead of us, circling those trees!"

"Long-billed curlew, my foot," Jeff muttered. "You're one slippery little fish, Kate Valera, but you're not going to get off the hook that easily."

"Aw, Mom!" Flannery lowered the binoculars in disgust. "That's not a curlew. It's just a dumb, old, brown pelican!"

"Well, keep a sharp lookout," Kate insisted, swinging the Jeep around the first grassy dune. "If you keep your eyes open, you can see all sorts of things!"

"Like mermaids!" Ellen chimed eagerly, and her father groaned.

Kate ignored him and kept on driving. She was through arguing with Jeff Parrish, she resolved. Two little girls deserved a good time, and she, for one, was going to see that they had it!

"Look, there's the water!" she announced as the Jeep rattled around the last curve in the road.

Flannery and Ellen cheered.

Chapter Seven

Jeff lay on a faded beach quilt, watching as Ellen and Flannery chased sandpipers along the frothy edge of the surf. The deli sandwiches, washed down with tangy iced lemonade, had been good to the last crumb. Kate's mango tarts—he'd eaten at least three of them—had all but melted on his tongue. He felt well fed, lazy and exquisitely contented.

Kate sat beside him, her feet off the quilt, her bare toes making little furrows in the warm, white sand. Only one thing, Jeff mused drowsily, would make the day more pleasant than it already was—to reach out, pull her down to him, and kiss her until both their heads spun.

For one delicious moment he contemplated doing just that—but no, he swiftly realized, a chaste kiss or two would never be enough to satisfy him. What he really wanted was to hold her close enough to feel every inch, every curve and hollow of her lovely body against his; to roll her in the sand, enmeshing their legs in a sweet, silken tangle as he—

Jeff bit back a surge of hot frustration. It wouldn't do to get carried away, he reminded himself. Not with their two little chaperones frolicking just down the beach. For now, at least, he would have to settle for something simple—like reaching for Kate's hand.

She tensed as his skin brushed hers. Jeff's pulse suspended itself for an instant, then plunged into a gallop as her trembling fingers uncurled in his palm, fitting into the lonely hollows as if they had been molded there. He held her hand gently, like a precious captive bird, not venturing to speak until, at last, the silence between them began to grow heavy.

"Thank you," he murmured, his fingers tightening around hers.

"Thank you for what?" Her voice carried a wary edge.

"For today. For this place and the mango tarts. For just being here."

"And for keeping a civil tongue in my head—don't forget that!" She laughed easily and naturally. "To tell the truth, Flannery almost had me convinced your mother was coming along. Fortunately for me, the little imp was joking."

"You needn't have worried," Jeff said. "My mother had other plans for the afternoon. She's on the committee for the new children's library here in Misty Point. They're having a get-together to tie up loose ends for the big fund-raising ball at the yacht club a week from Saturday. Have you heard about it?"

"I have." Her fingers slipped away, leaving Jeff's hand empty as she drew her feet up, wrapped her arms around her knees and stared out at the waves. "One of the gallery owners asked me to donate a small pot for the auction. I plan to drop it off Saturday morning and pick it up the next day if it doesn't sell. Any more questions?"

"Well, yes. I was hoping you'd agree to go with me."

Something hard glimmered in her eyes. "No," she said. "That affair is for summer people."

"What are you talking about? The library is for the whole town."

"I know. And it's going to be wonderful, especially for bright kids like my own daughter. It's just the idea that the visitors are doing this for the townspeople..." Her voice trailed off into a sigh.

"Are you saying it feels like charity?"

"Oh...sort of, I guess. It's as if the summer folks are saying, 'Let's get together and do something nice for the poor, backward natives.' With that attitude, it's hard for the rest of us not to feel like we're being patronized. And this isn't just personal, Jeff. Most of the year-round people feel the same way."

"Oh, come on!" Jeff worked his elbows beneath him and pushed himself up beside her, giving up on romance for the moment. "Hey—summer kids read, too. Everybody will benefit from the library!"

Kate's eyes shot blue-green darts. "Then why isn't 'everybody' involved in the fund-raising? Why does the Misty Point Children's Library Committee roster read like a who's who list out of *Town and Country?*"

"I think you're suffering from a bad case of reverse snobbery," Jeff said.

"No—come on, just think about it. Who's on your mother's committee?"

"Let's see," Jeff mused reluctantly. "She mentioned that Mrs. Bodell is in charge. Then there's Mrs. Appleton and Mrs. Carling..." He trailed off, his silence conceding that she was right.

"See?" Her expressive fingers stabbed the air. "It's become a social thing, a nice little excuse for bored, wealthy people to dress up and spend money! Why should they care about—''

''Whoa, there!'' Half-amused by her fervor, he laid a restraining hand on her arm. ''Give some credit where it's due, Kate. What have the year-round people done about their own library fund-raising?''

Kate glared at him indignantly, then sighed as his reasoning sank home. ''All right, nothing. Misty Point isn't exactly a wealthy town. But that doesn't mean we don't want to help. It's just that nobody's asked us to get involved.''

''Well…'' Jeff mused out loud as the germ of an idea began to sprout in his mind, ''maybe it's time someone from the town spoke up.''

''Like who?'' Her eyes challenged him, then widened as she realized what he had in mind. ''Oh, no, you don't! Not me!''

''And why not?''

''Because I have no political clout. And because I have all the diplomatic skills of a wounded bobcat—or is that something you have yet to discover about me?''

''Do I have to answer that?'' Jeff's eyes rolled skyward in a parody of innocence, and Kate chuckled.

''All right, I'll let you off this time,'' she said. ''And I'll give you credit for a good suggestion. Charlene Hornaday, the mayor, is open to new ideas. I'll pay her a call. She'll take it from there.''

''Chicken.'' Jeff nudged her ribs with a teasing fingertip.

''*What* did you call me?'' She stared at him, bristling like a startled cat.

''You heard what I called you.'' He watched her lazily, relishing the play of color in her eyes and cheeks. ''You're passing the buck, Ms. Kathryn Valera. By rights, you should jump in and get involved yourself. Isn't that what your passionate hero, Howard Roark, would have done?''

"Look, I already explained…" She had her feet under her now, ready to spring up and stalk away. Then she saw his grinning face and realized he was baiting her. "Oh!" she sputtered. "Oh, you—you beastly…"

In a flash she was sprinting toward the waves. Her feet spattered the white surf as she snatched up Flannery's abandoned sand pail and scooped it full of seawater.

Ellen and Flannery had stopped their games to watch. They shrieked with laughter as Kate charged up the beach and flung the bucket squarely at Jeff, drenching him from head to toe.

He staggered comically to his feet, water dripping off his eyebrows, nose and chin. "Oh-ho!" he boomed, playing to the audience in his deepest Papa Bear voice. "So you want to get rough, do you?"

Catching Kate off guard, he made a lightning-quick lunge, seized her by the waist and swung her up against his chest.

"Don't you dare…" She kicked and struggled, half furious, half laughing, pummeling his chest with helpless, glancing blows. The girls danced around them, whooping like gleeful little savages.

"You're going to get the dunking you deserve, and then some," he muttered as he carried her toward the water. He felt the gritty wet sand beneath his feet, and then the first wave swirling around his ankles. He would carry her deeper, he resolved—not only to get her good and wet, but also to make sure her delicate skin didn't get bumped or scraped when he tossed her into the surf.

The only trouble was, as they went deeper, he couldn't see where he was going. He struggled for a foothold in the treacherously shifting sand, took a step and crunched his

toe against a rock. As he staggered, cursing the pain, a
walrus-sized swell from the wake of a passing power boat
came rolling across the inlet. Jeff glimpsed its approach,
but not in time to recover his balance. The wave struck him
sideways, sweeping his legs out from under him. Top-
heavy with Kate in his arms, he capsized and sank like a
waterlogged schooner.

Kate pushed for the surface as he let her go. An instant
later, Jeff's own head broke into the sunlight. He saw the
girls dog-paddling giddily in the ripples from the spent
wave. He saw Kate standing waist-deep, dripping and
laughing, her skin glittering with sunlit drops of water.

She reached out for the girls and drew them toward her.
The three of them clung together, giggling hysterically as
Jeff sputtered and sneezed to clear the seawater out of his
nose.

"Daddy—you're funny!" Ellen gasped between spasms
of laughter. "You ought to be a clown—like Jo-Jo!"

"Funny, am I?" He charged the trio, bulldozing through
the water. "*Funny,* am I? I'll show you funny!" He
launched himself at Kate's legs, bent on overturning them
all, but she was too slippery and agile for him. She bobbed
out of his reach, clutching their daughters and grinning like
an imp.

Into the game now, Jeff lunged after them again. That
was when a second swell, half again the size of the previous
one, struck him from behind. The momentum slammed him
into Kate and the girls, sweeping them all toward the beach.

The girls squealed as they tumbled onto the sand. Seconds later, the wave had retreated, leaving the four of them
drenched and gasping at the water's edge.

Ellen was shaken. Her lower lip quivered as she glanced
at her father, seeking reassurance. Jeff was about to reach
for her when Flannery began to laugh.

"Look at us!" she giggled. "Beached whales! Two big ones and two little ones! Four skinny, floppy beached whales!"

The corners of Ellen's mouth twitched into a tentative smile. A tiny chuckle materialized from her throat, and then, suddenly, she was laughing too.

"And look at you!" Kate hooted, pointing at Jeff's coated chest and legs. "You're a—a hairy sand monster!"

"Well you look like a drowned rat, and you've got seaweed growing out of your—uh..." Jeff struggled to control himself as Kate glanced down and discovered a string of kelp sprouting from the cleavage between her breasts. She drew it out inch by inch, tugging at its unbelievable length until she collapsed on the sand in a fit of helpless giggles.

They laughed, the four of them together on the sun-sparkled beach. They laughed until the tears ran down their faces, until they lay exhausted and spent with silliness.

Nothing in his life, Jeff reflected, had ever felt so right.

Kate walked out of the Hornaday Real Estate and Insurance Office blinking in the afternoon glare as the past fifteen minutes replayed in her mind like a clip from a B-grade horror movie.

You idiot! she berated herself. All you had to do was say no. One simple word, and you'd have been off the hook! Just *N-O*, NO!

At least that *might* have worked, she groused as she shuffled to the curb where the Jeep was parked. The only trouble was, saying no to Charlene Hornaday, Misty Point's energetic mayor, was like saying no to a steam roller.

"Nonsense, dear, you'd be perfect for the job!" Charlene's age-splotched hands, glittering with faux diamond rings, had clasped Kate's in a determined grip. "Why, you're a well-known artist! The whole community respects you! Now, there's no use arguing—my mind is made up. I'm going to call Mrs. Bodell right now and tell her you'll be attending all the fund-raising committee's functions as the official representative of Misty Point's year-round community! Now, don't go away—this'll only take a minute!''

Mercifully the Bodells' line had been busy on the first try, and then Charlene had gotten another call. In the interim, Kate had managed to excuse herself and slink out the door. But the mayor would follow through, all right. Once Charlene Hornaday got a bit in her teeth, there was no stopping her.

"So what did she say, Mom?" Flannery was sitting in the back seat of the Jeep, scribbling intently in her mermaid notebook.

"I'll tell you on the way home." Kate's fingers quivered hesitantly on the door handle. Jeff would laugh, she reminded herself. This was exactly the kind of thing that would amuse his cynical mind—Kate Valera on the hot seat again. For all she knew, he could have had a hand in—

Kate went bolt rigid as the possibility struck her. No, he wouldn't have. He couldn't have—

"What's the matter, Mom?" Flannery asked.

"Nothing, honey," Kate fibbed. "I, uh, just have to make a quick phone call. Hang on."

She strode back up the street to the booth outside the drugstore, fished for a quarter in her purse and, with shaking fingers, jammed it into the slot.

Jeff would likely be working, she reminded herself as she punched the number buttons and waited for the first ring. He had been immersed in the new plans for the hospital wing—but not too immersed to give her several warm, tender phone calls over the weekend.

Even now, the very thought of those phone calls made her knees go mushy. It wasn't so much what he said. No, it was more the way he *listened*—listened to every drab little detail of her day, to her most trivial concerns and her wildest hopes. He made her feel so cherished, so cared for, that it was all too easy to believe their relationship would last.

But she was only a summer diversion, Kate reminded herself angrily. Jeff Parrish was playing with her. He was manipulating her like a toy. And this time he'd gone too far!

"Hello?"

His voice went through her like sunlight through wild honey. Kate steeled herself against his power to soften her.

"Tell me you didn't do it," she said. "I'm not saying I'll believe you, but tell me, anyway. I want to find out whether you've got the bald-faced nerve to say it."

There was a tick of stunned silence on the other end of the line. She heard him take a deep breath.

"Kate, I have no idea what you're talking about," he said.

"Try Mayor Hornaday. Try the diabolical notion that only *you* would have put into her head."

"Mayor..." His breath caught; then he muttered something Kate was just as grateful she couldn't understand. "Look," he said. "I don't know what's happened, but, so help me, I've had no contact with your mayor. I've never met her, never phoned her, never written to her—Kate, I swear on my honor, I don't know what you're talking about."

The ring of sincerity in his voice pierced Kate's defensive armor as no words could. Limp with embarrassment, she slumped against the wall of the phone booth. "You mean," she said slowly, "you had nothing to do with her decision to appoint me to the fund-raising committee?"

Jeff made a little choking noise that sounded suspiciously like a laugh.

"It isn't funny!" Kate hissed. "Jeff, what am I going to do?"

"Well," he drawled, his voice spiked with ill-concealed amusement, "you can always chicken out and resign."

"After the speech I gave Charlene about the need for the whole town to get involved? I'd never have the nerve to show my face in Misty Point again!"

"Well, in that case, I have a better idea."

"What?" she challenged him, bracing herself for his answer.

"Make the most of it, lady. Put on your flashiest dress and come with me to the yacht club party on Saturday."

Kate had sensed what was coming. All the same, she felt her stomach clench. "Jeff, it's not that simple," she muttered. "I can't just—"

"Come on—you're on the committee!"

"But how will the committee accept me? What about Mrs. Bodell? I turned her little girl into a painted clown at Ellen's party. What about your mother, for heaven's sake? I know what she thinks of me!"

"Kate…" The flicker of hesitation in his voice only confirmed her fears. "Don't let these people intimidate you," he said.

"I'm not intimidated. Not by anyone."

"Then prove it."

Kate felt the trap closing around her, and she knew there was no graceful way out. She took a deep breath, her pulse racing as if she were about to plunge over the edge of a cliff. "All right," she said, "if that's what it takes to convince you."

"You don't have to convince me of anything. I'm delighted you're coming with me."

"You may change your mind before this is over."

"I'll take that chance," he said. "And, by the way—"

"What?"

He chuckled warmly, deep in his throat. "Just in case you have any doubts, I'm truly looking forward to this. When I walk into that place with you on my arm...lady, we're going to knock their socks off!"

Jeff was still smiling when he hung up the phone. Kate made him smile. She made him laugh. She made him think. True, there were times when she also made him want to grind his teeth and yank his hair; but even that was all right. He felt alive again—more alive than he had ever felt in his uptight, constricted life.

But could it last? That was a question he was not even ready to ask.

The smile faded as he crossed the room to stand at the open window, gazing out toward the dunes. He had not planned on Kate Valera. She had blown into his life like an unexpected summer squall, shaking him loose from his safe moorings and sweeping him into the unbridled sea.

He was in way over his head with Kate—that much he already knew. And he knew he wanted her. He wanted her in his arms and in his bed. He wanted her in his life and in Ellen's.

But wanting something didn't make it fitting, or even practical. He had always prided himself on making choices with his head, not his heart. He had always done the right thing, the proper thing.

So why now, of all times, was his heart threatening a full-scale mutiny?

Ever since that day on the beach, a dream had been creeping into his mind at unguarded moments. A family dream, with a father, a mother and two little girls—and there was someone else in the dream, a small, sweet, brand-new someone with love ties to them all....

The dream was nothing more than an idle fantasy, Jeff told himself—a will-o'-the-wisp spun from his own loneliness. Kate had done wonders in easing his pain and Ellen's, but what had he done for her? What could he offer her except disappointment and frustration?

"Daddy?" Ellen had walked softly into the studio, clutching the pink conch shell Flannery had given her. Her face wore the troubled look Jeff had come to recognize so well in the past eighteen months.

"What's up, honey?" he asked gently.

"Why doesn't Grandma like Kate and Flannery?"

Jeff bit back a groan as the question rocked him. Not that it came as a surprise. His mother had made no secret of her hostility toward Kate. All the same, it dismayed him that she would be so frank with Ellen.

He bent his knees into a crouch, bringing his face down to a level with his daughter's. "How do you know Grandma doesn't like them?" he asked. "Did she tell you?"

She shook her head. "I heard her on the phone with Mrs. Bodell just now. She was saying something about that awful Jo-Jo woman and her little red-haired brat." A tear spilled between Ellen's dark lashes to leave a glistening trail down her cheek. "Kate isn't awful, Daddy. She's the nicest lady I know. And Flannery is my best friend forever and ever."

Jeff's hand tightened on his daughter's shoulder as a hot tide of emotion welled up in his throat. He owed his mother more than he could ever repay, he reminded himself. But it wasn't enough. He couldn't just sit back and let her hurt Kate.

"Why doesn't Grandma like them, Daddy?" Ellen asked again, more plaintively this time.

"It's not that she doesn't like them, honey," Jeff explained as gently as he could. "She just doesn't understand them, that's all. People tend to fear what they don't understand."

"Well, can't we *make* her understand?"

Jeff pushed himself to his feet, knowing he could not put off the confrontation any longer. "Maybe we can—maybe we can't. Whatever happens, I'm about to try."

"Let's go downstairs and find her." Ellen tugged at Jeff's wrist. "Come on, I'll help you talk to her, Daddy."

"Sorry, doll." Tenderly he peeled away her small, clinging fingers. "This is something your old dad needs to do by himself. You wait up here, and we'll go out for pizza later. Okay?"

"Okay." Ellen picked up a sketch pad she'd left on Jeff's desk earlier that day and curled up in the leather armchair.

"No listening. Promise?"

"Promise." Her pencil was already roughing out the long fish tail of a mermaid. Jeff walked out of the studio, closed the door behind him and strode resolutely down the stairs. The next few minutes would not be pleasant, but there were things that needed to be said, and they could not wait any longer.

He found his mother seated at the dining room table, checking off entries on a long list of names and addresses— the guest list for the fund-raiser, he assumed. Her face wore an irritated scowl.

"Is something wrong?" He slid out a chair and seated himself on the opposite side of the table.

"Yes," she snapped, her pen slashing across the paper.

"And my intuition tells me you just might know something about it, Jefferson."

"Try me." Jeff leaned back and tried to look detached, knowing she wasn't fooled.

"It's that Jo-Jo woman—"

"Her name is Kate, Mother."

"Well, whatever her name is, she's really done it this time! Cozying up to the mayor! Insinuating herself onto the fund-raising committee—"

"Now wait a minute," Jeff interrupted sharply. "In the first place, being on the committee wasn't Kate's idea—she didn't even want the job, but the mayor insisted she take it. In the second place, what's wrong with her being on the committee? You need some representation from the town."

"Oh, perhaps. But Jefferson, dear, surely not *her!*"

"And why not?" Jeff's voice crackled with suppressed anger. His mother stared at him, then tossed down her pen. It clattered across the table and rolled off the edge.

"Has the woman bewitched you that much? Can't you see that she's as common as grass?"

"Mother, I—"

"No, listen to me. She lives alone with her daughter—no sign of any other family—in that trashy, isolated little house, doing heaven knows what—"

"Kate's an artist, and a fine one!" Jeff retorted. "Her work is displayed all over town!"

"All right, so she does ceramics—a nice little hobby but no respectable way to make a living. As for putting on that ridiculous clown getup and making a spectacle of herself—"

"The money she makes as Jo-Jo goes into her daughter's college fund." Jeff fought back his swelling temper.

"And I suppose the moon is made of green cheese!" his

mother snorted disdainfully. "Come down to earth, Jefferson. I have it on good authority that the woman waits on tables at the Pancake Palace. My son—my precious, only son—is dating a common *waitress* who probably—"

"That's enough." The cold anger in Jeff's voice would have stopped a charging she-bear. The ceiling fan whirred in the afternoon silence as his mother stared at him across the table.

"I know what Kate does," he said. "It's hard, honest work. There's no shame in it—and there's no shame in *her*. Kathryn Valera is one of the finest women I've ever known."

Her eyes bulged as if he had just struck her in the breast with a parlor dart. "Well!" she huffed, fanning herself furiously with the pages of the guest list. "If I didn't credit you with more sense, Jefferson, I could almost be convinced you'd fallen in love with the woman! As it is, I'll chalk it up to a passing case of silly schoolboy infatuation and trust you'll get over it!"

"I have no plans to get over it." Beneath his veneer of icy calm, Jeff's emotions were churning like steam pistons. "I'm in love with Kate. She's been wonderful for me and wonderful for Ellen—"

"You call drawing those foolish fairy-tale pictures wonderful? Why, if you ask me—"

"I'm not asking you this time, Mother—only warning you. If you're as wise as I hope, you'll stop putting Kate down and start building a good relationship with her. The library committee is a good place to start. Otherwise—"

"Why, Jefferson!" she gasped, her fingers fluttering to her throat. "I do believe you're threatening me!"

"No, my dearest lady, it's not meant to be a threat—not unless you force me to choose. I love you, Mother, and I'm grateful for all you've done. But if Kate will have me—

and there's no certainty of that—I want to make her and her little girl a permanent part of our lives."

"No!" She was on her feet, her chest and chin thrusting like the prow of the *Q.E. II.* "I won't tolerate such a notion! We have certain standards in this family—standards of quality and breeding, and I won't have you defiling our—"

"Mother," Jeff sighed wearily, "with all due respect, Adolf Hitler had standards of quality and breeding, too. But that didn't mean he was right."

"Oh!" The air hissed in and out of her imposing chest. *"Oh!"* She turned away without another word, strode out of the room and stalked indignantly up the stairs. An instant later Jeff heard the door of her room slam shut.

He had said too much, Jeff realized as he sat numbly at the table. He had let his anger push hidden emotions to the surface and form them into words. He had never before said that he loved Kate or wanted to marry her—not even to himself. But now, as he stared down at his shaking hands, he knew it was true.

Feisty little Kate Valera was the woman he loved with all his soul. She was the woman he wanted to mother his children, to stand at his side, to share his life and fortunes forever.

If he could make it work.

If he could fight his way through the barricades of prejudice, fear, pride and insecurity that loomed on all sides of them.

"Daddy?"

Jeff glanced up to see Ellen huddled on the landing, her silver eyes big with questions.

"Hey, I thought I told you to stay put," he said.

"I did. Then I heard Grandma's door slam. Is she mad?"

"I'm afraid so." Jeff eased himself away from the table

and stood up as Ellen's pink tennis shoes pattered down the hardwood stairs.

"I knew it," she sighed. "You should've let me help you. Grandma doesn't get so mad when I talk to her."

"Don't worry about it. She'll be fine," Jeff muttered, doubting the strength of his own words. "Hey, how about that pizza I promised you?"

"Can we go to Gepetto's?" She scampered down the last few steps to catch his hand with her warm little fingers.

"We can go anywhere you like." Jeff swung her arm, half-distracted, as they strolled out the door.

"Daddy, can I ask you a question?" she ventured as he buckled her into the back seat.

"I suppose so."

"You won't get mad?"

"Should I?" A warning light flickered in Jeff's head as his daughter mulled over her reply.

"Maybe," she admitted at last. "But promise you won't, all right?"

"All right, I promise."

"And you'll still take me for pizza?" Her eyes were uncertain, like an anxious puppy's.

"Hmm. This sounds like serious business." Jeff tweaked her chin, hoping it wasn't. "All right, I won't get mad, and I'll still take you for pizza. Now let's hear your question."

Ellen squirmed against her seat belt, then took a deep gulp of air. "Daddy?"

"Uh-huh?" Jeff waited.

"Who was Adolf Hitler?"

Chapter Eight

The red message light on Kate's answering machine was blinking when she walked into the house. She hesitated, then plopped her bag of groceries onto the counter and punched the Play bar. Maybe it was good news—the agency with another gig for Jo-Jo, or better yet, a gallery owner with an offer on one of her pots.

Alas, it was neither.

"Kate, dear," a syrupy female voice oozed out of the speaker. "This is Lacy Ann Bodell—Congressman Ennis Bodell's wife. I just got off the phone with your mayor—what a cunning idea, appointing you to our little fund-raising committee. I wanted to be the very first to call and welcome you! I confess I've been wanting to meet you ever since the party for that poor little Parrish girl. Muffet had such amusing things to say about your performance that day...."

Battling the urge to grind her teeth, Kate forced herself to hear the entire message. It was couched in exquisitely polite terms, but only a fool could have missed its catty, condescending tone. By the time she allowed her finger to jab the Erase button, her temper was seething like four-alarm chili on a hot stove.

How could she go through with this?

Then again, how could she *not* go through with it?

How could she slink away like a coward and leave the field to the Mrs. Bodells and Mrs. Parrishes of Misty Point? What would that say to the mayor, to the townspeople and, most important of all, to Flannery?

What would it say to Jeff?

"Mom?" Flannery had come bouncing into the kitchen with a second bag of groceries. "If I clean my room, can I invite Ellen over to watch the *Swan Lake* video tonight?"

"Oh, so it's bribery now, is it? I'll tell you what—clean your room. Then we'll see."

"But I want to phone her now," Flannery persisted. "Ellen's grandma says it isn't polite to call and invite people at the last minute."

Kate sighed, fighting the black weight that balled in her stomach at the very mention of Jeff's formidable mother. "All right. First you can help me put away the groceries. Then you can call Ellen, and *then* you're to go right in and clean your room. Deal?"

"Deal!" Flannery grinned and began tossing vegetables into the crisper.

"Don't bruise the tomatoes—they're expensive," Kate cautioned as she reached up to stock a shelf with cans of cat food. She envied Flannery's fearlessness in the face of judgment and rejection. Once, she remembered, she had been just as open and trusting. But that had been a long time ago.

"Ellen's grandma isn't really a mean person, you know," Flannery remarked as if reading her mind. "She's just unhappy and scared. She's afraid of being old and alone, with nobody needing her. That's why she's so nervous about you and me.''

"And how did you figure all this out, Miss People-Expert?'' Kate asked, laughing to hide her astonishment at her daughter's insight.

"It shows in her face. Anybody can see it." Flannery tossed her a jar of peppercorns intended for the spice shelf. "So what are you going to wear to the fund-raiser?"

"Wear?" Kate dropped the jar. It bounced onto the floor and rolled under the kitchen table. Flannery scrambled after it as Kate stood blinking into space. Not until this minute had it occurred to her that she had absolutely nothing to wear to a formal event.

"I'll bet you're going to look gorgeous!" Flannery's voice floated from under the table. "I'll bet Ellen's dad will take one look and beg you to marry him!"

Kate groaned. "Sweetheart, this isn't one of your fairy stories. Things like that don't happen in real life."

"But wouldn't you *like* it to happen? Wouldn't you like being married to a rich, handsome man who adored you?" Flannery came up with the peppercorns, grinning like a diver who'd just found a piece of the *Atocha* treasure. "Well, *wouldn't* you?" she demanded.

"You're pushing it, young lady!" Kate snatched the jar from her hand and turned to a furious rearranging of the spice cupboard. "I know you mean well, Flannery, but there's no use getting your hopes up. You'll only be disappointed."

"Maybe." The grin remained in place, as if she were privy to some great secret. "I've put away all the stuff I can reach. Is it okay if I call Ellen now?"

"Go ahead—we can pick her up and bring her home if need be. Just make sure it's all right with her father—and her grandmother.''

Kate closed the cupboard doors, wandered into the living room and sank wearily onto the sofa. Mehitabel uncoiled from among the cushions and crept, purring, onto her lap. Ecstatic quivers rippled through the cat's plump body as she worked her needle claws in and out, in and out, against Kate's denim-clad thighs.

Something to wear. Kate rubbed the satiny ears as her mind ticked off every outdated, shabby, pathetic item in her wardrobe. She wanted to look her best—as much for Jeff as for herself, but nothing she owned was appropriate. Nothing even came close.

In the shopping center where she'd done her last Jo-Jo gig, someone had opened an upscale dress shop. There was one gown, a simple but elegant jade green chiffon she'd admired in the window—

But who was she kidding? The dress was almost four hundred dollars, and she'd all but cleaned out her checking account buying this week's groceries. She had never believed in charge accounts or possessed a credit card. Right now, in fact, the only money she had was the $5,120 in Flannery's college fund. Maybe she could borrow enough to—

No. It was out of the question. She had sworn she would never touch that money, and she could not break her promise now—especially for something as frivolous as a party gown.

There had to be an answer, she lectured herself. *There was always an answer.* Her grandmother had taught her that axiom when she was small, and Kate had never forgotten it. But where was the solution now? If only her grandmother were here—

Then Kate remembered the funeral dress.

She had no idea how old that dress was or where it had come from. Her grandmother had worn it for as long as she could remember—but only to funerals. To show respect, the old woman had explained.

As a child Kate had been awed by the dress's elegance. Its fabric was a deep black silk bombazine, embroidered with tiny jet beads on the bodice and hem. It lay folded in tissue paper now, at the bottom of an old steamer trunk in Kate's studio, still in fine condition. Her grandmother had been a large woman. Kate knew the dress would fit her like a tent, but she was handy with a sewing machine, and there was plenty of fabric for remodeling.

Yes, it had to be the answer.

She could only hope her grandmother, heaven rest her soul, would understand.

"Ellen can come over at seven!" Flannery danced into the living room, spinning pirouettes around the coffee table. "And we won't even have to pick her up. Her dad is going to bring her. Will you help me bake some chocolate chip cookies?"

"*If* that room of yours is clean in time." Kate stood up, spilling the cat to the floor. It made no difference that Jeff was coming over, she assured herself as she brushed the coarse orange fur off her jeans. The prospect of seeing him again was no reason for her heart to take wing like a happy swallow and burst into a soaring explosion of dips and barrel rolls.

So why was it happening?

She was a fool to get misty-eyed over a man like Jeff Parrish, she told herself as she wrestled the aging vacuum cleaner out of the closet and jammed the plug into the wall outlet. That day at the beach, with everyone laughing and happy, she had given in to the magic. For a time as brief as a rainbow, she had almost let herself believe he could love her. She had almost let herself believe the four of them could be a family, she and Jeff and their two little girls.

But it was time to grow up and face reality. For all the tenderness he'd shown her, Jeff had to know that he was out of her league—way out. Even if he was temporarily asleep to that fact, his mother certainly wasn't.

And his mother wasn't the only problem.

He was a wealthy snob—she hated snobbery with a passion.

His life was rule bound—she treasured the freedom to be spontaneous.

Her life was here, in Misty Point—he was only on vacation.

Then there was the fantasy problem. And more. So much more.

For any one of a dozen reasons, they were headed on a collision course for the rocks. If she had any sense at all, she would jump ship now, before the inevitable crash. No matter how she felt about Jeff, she could not go on pretending everything was wonderful, with no end in sight. There were too many vulnerable hearts that would be crushed when the relationship ran aground.

Kate's emotions blackened like the clouds of an incoming storm as she worked the wheezing vacuum cleaner over the threadbare Persian rug. What was the matter with her, thinking she could remodel a decades-old dress into a fashionable ball gown and mingle with the laughing, elegant summer people as if she belonged? She was just like the Little Mermaid—longing for legs to dance with her prince, abandoning who and what she was to glimpse a world that could never be hers.

Break it off now—tonight, before she changed her mind—that was the only thing to do. As soon as the girls were settled with the video and cookies, she would ask to speak with Jeff in private. Then she would summon all her courage and do the right thing.

She could go to the fund-raiser alone, if she had to. Better yet, she could fake some emergency and avoid showing up at all. Why not? Why leave herself open to more hurt and humiliation?

Switching off the vacuum, Kate drifted to the window and stood gazing out at a lone albatross winging its way above the dunes. There were far worse things than being on her own, she reminded herself—after all, she hadn't managed too badly over the years. But being with Jeff had given her a taste of what she had missed—a taste as fleeting as the sweetness of honey on her tongue.

It would not be easy letting go.

Mehitabel slunk out of her hiding place under the sofa to rub her sinuous warmth against Kate's legs. Kate reached down and scooped the cat into her arms. As she furrowed her fingers through the thick, satiny fur, a single tear welled in her eye, spilled over the lid and glided silently down her cheek.

The doorbell rang promptly at seven, just as Kate was lifting the last sheet of chocolate chip cookies out of the oven. She forced herself to move slowly, ignoring the leap of her pulse as Flannery bounded toward the door and flung it open.

Jeff's presence filled the house like the scent of pine at Christmastime. Kate felt it even before she saw or heard him, and she ached inside with the pain of the loss to come.

The girls squealed with the pleasure of being together, startling the cat into a hasty retreat under the kitchen table. Reining in her own eagerness, Kate stuck doggedly to her task. She would see Jeff soon enough—and soon enough he would be gone for good.

She was laying the cookies on a wire rack to cool when he came walking lightly into the kitchen. She held her breath, quivering as his arms slid around her from behind, drawing her against him. "I see there's a plate in the living room for the girls. Are all these for me?" he asked, his breath tickling her ear.

"They're to share—but only if you're a very good boy."

"I'm always a good boy." His lips brushed the bare curve of her neck. "Just let me get you alone, and I'll show you how good I can be."

Kate stiffened against him, fighting the freshets of heat that surged through her body. "The girls..." she murmured shakily.

"They're busy." His hands slid up her rib cage beneath her loose-fitting black cotton sweater. Kate closed her eyes, wanting his touch on her skin—everywhere—wanting his kisses and his love—wanting to be his, completely and forever. Wanting it all—and knowing that she might as well be reaching for the sun.

"Behave yourself!" She spun away from him with a playful little laugh. "Here, have a nice, warm cookie!"

She had meant to shove the cookie in his mouth, but it crumbled in her hand and plopped onto the linoleum. Grateful for the distraction, she grabbed a paper towel and bent to clean up the mess.

"Why do I have the distinct feeling you're avoiding me?" Jeff asked, wetting another towel and crouching to help her.

Kate stared at the floor, not trusting herself to meet his eyes.

"Do you need to talk?" he asked.

Kate's heart lurched. "Uh-huh," she said. "*We* need to talk. But in private. Not here."

His eyes flashed, but he masked his emotions with a smile as he helped her to her feet. "Hey, what's with the gloomy face? Did somebody die?"

"Not exactly." She turned away and fumbled for the
spatula again, burning her thumb on the hot edge of the
cookie sheet. The pain triggered a surge of tears. She struggled to blink them away as she scraped blindly at the re-
maining cookies on the sheet.

"Kate?" He caught her chin, forcing her face toward the
light. "Blast it, is it something I've done?"

"No," she whispered, stung by the genuine concern in
his voice. "It's nothing you've done. Come on, let's go
outside. The girls will be all right in here for a little while."

"Lead the way. You never know—I just might have a
few things to say to you, too."

She let him follow her through the dim clutter of the
pottery studio, fighting the temptation to reach back and
take his hand. Why did he have to make this so hard on
her? If he were crass, insensitive or blatantly fickle, like so
many men she knew, it would be a pleasure to show him
the exit. Why did Jefferson Parrish have to be so
damned...wonderful?

Kate's hands shook as she worked the bolt open on the
little-used back door. Jeff waited quietly in the shadows
behind her as the haunting strains of Tchaikovsky drifted
from the living room. What was he thinking? Did he know
her heart was about to break? Would he care?

The bolt gave way with a rusty click. Kate nudged the
door with her shoulder. It creaked open like the lid of a
jewel box—revealing the most glorious sunset she had ever
seen.

Layered clouds, blazing hues of gold, tangerine, vermil-
ion and mauve, streaked like tattered gossamer ribbons
from horizon to horizon. It was as if Corot, Turner and
van Gogh had somehow collided, spilling their heavenly
paint boxes across the sky. Forgetting herself for an instant,

Kate stumbled out into the twilight, her lips parted in wonder.

"I ordered it just for us. What do you think?" Jeff's arms slid around her from behind. His freshly razored chin brushed her temple as he spoke.

"How much did you have to pay?" Kate murmured, struggling to resist the prickly warmth of his breath in her ear.

"Not much. Just a nickel and my soul."

"I'd say you got the best of the...bargain." Her breath caught as his hands slipped beneath her sweater again, his fingers tracing an electric path along the top edge of her jeans. Time seemed to stop as the sky deepened to tones of crimson, violet and indigo. Then the world spun like a child's rainbow top as he turned Kate in his arms to capture her all-too-eager lips with his own.

All her wise intentions evaporated, sizzling like raindrops on molten lava in the heat of their embrace. Her mouth softened and parted, ravenous for the honey-velvet feel of his tongue. Her fingers raked his thick hair. Nothing made sense in her spinning mind except the awareness that she was his—that she wanted Jeff Parrish more than air, more than sunlight, more than life.

She moaned as his thumb eased below the waistband of her jeans to brush the exquisitely sensitive hollow of her navel. Lingering, his hand paused for the space of a breath, then slipped upward to caress her ribs—and upward still to skim the lace-edged cup of her bra. His touch on her breast sent waves of hot sensation rocketing through Kate's body. She whimpered, the sound awakening her to a sudden surge of panic.

"No..." she gasped. "Jeff, that's enough—"

His breath rasped out in a long exhalation as he withdrew his hand and gathered her into a chaste, gentle embrace.

She huddled against him, shaken by the power of her own desire.

"Maybe we'd better go back inside," she whispered, but he only pulled her closer against him.

"Kate..." His heartbeat drummed against her ear. "I'm in love with you. Don't you know that?"

His words, so longed for, triggered a second burst of panic in Kate—this one exploding from so deep inside her that she went weak with its pain. "Stop!" she hissed, pulling away from him. "Don't you see it only makes things harder when you talk like that?"

Jeff's hands dropped to his sides. The sky behind him cast a soft amber glow on his hair. "All I see is a beautiful, frightened woman," he said. "What's wrong, Kate? I'm here, and I'm willing to listen, but I can't even do that unless you'll talk to me."

When she hesitated, he reached out and caught her hand. "Come on, let's walk," he said.

They drifted, fingers interlaced, toward the dunes, the rushing sigh of the waves echoing faintly in their ears. Kate struggled to speak, but her thoughts had bottlenecked somewhere between her mind and her emotion-choked throat.

"You're afraid I'm going to spout pretty words, make a few promises and then leave? Is that it?" Jeff asked.

Kate nodded mutely, wishing it were that simple.

"It doesn't have to be that way, you know," he said, his fingers tightening around hers. "We have a chance, you and I. We can make it, but I can't go the whole distance alone. You've got to meet me at least partway."

"And offer myself on a platter to be pecked to pieces by your mother and her friends?"

"They're just people—some of them good, some of them weak and frightened. There's no reason to let them intimidate you."

"That's easy enough for you to say. You grew up with them." Kate closed her eyes, letting the evening wind feather her hair back from her damp face. Why couldn't she just open up and tell Jeff everything? He would walk away in disgust, she knew. But at least he would understand.

"What are you really afraid of, Kate?" The question recalled memories of another night, another beach.

"What am I afraid of?" Kate struggled to forge the truth into words. "That I'll let myself love you, and you'll leave. Or even worse, that you won't leave—and you'll end up being ashamed of me."

His hands caught her shoulders and spun her around to face him. "Kate, I could never—"

"Don't you understand?" she flared. "I don't belong in your world—and even if I could belong, I wouldn't. I don't *want* to be like those people...."

His arms gathered her close again. This time he held her gently, rocking her like a child. "My dear, sweet Kate," he murmured, his lips stirring her hair. "How could I ask you to be like anyone else when I love you so much the way you are? I love everything about you—your integrity, your spirit, your fire...."

Kate nestled against him, letting his words wash over her like warm spring rain. Jeff loved her—loved *her*. And if there was a chance for them, any chance at all, she had to take it. But first she would have to be absolutely honest with him.

"I need to go to Raleigh in the morning," he was saying. "The hospital board is meeting and wants to look at my design for the new wing. This is it, Kate, the moment of truth."

Kate looked up into his earnest face, her eyes caressing

every line, plane, crease and hollow. "They'll love your plans," she whispered. "They've got to!"

"I hope you're right." He gave her a quick, hard hug. "I'll be back Saturday evening in time to take you to the fund-raiser."

"Jeff—"

"Oh, no you don't!" He gave her chin a playful tweak. "No cold feet allowed, Ms. Kathryn Valera. If the board approves my design, I'll be in the mood to celebrate. And I'll be the proudest man alive when I walk into the yacht club with you on my arm."

She slumped against him, suddenly fearful again. "It's not just cold feet," she declared, dreading what she knew had to come next. "Before we take this any further, there's something you need to know about me—something you're not going to like."

"Try me." His arms slipped around her once more.

Kate swallowed, groping for a way to begin. "It's a very long story, but it has to be told. After you've heard it, I'll understand if you want to walk away and never—"

A nerve-shattering yowl cut her off in mid-sentence. The cry, which had burst from a nearby thicket of oleanders, swiftly erupted into a hellish cacophony of growls, wails and hisses.

"Oh, no—Mehitabel!" Kate spun away from Jeff and plunged frantically into the bushes, the sharp twigs grabbing at her sweater.

Two furry forms, one light and one dark, fought and tumbled in the shadows. As she reached them, the darker one broke loose and tore away into the night, leaving Mehitabel, spitting like a fury, to be snatched up in Kate's arms.

"There…there…it's all right, baby." Kate soothed the cat, who was puffed to half again her usual size and still hissing.

"Is she hurt?" Jeff had caught up with her.

"I—don't know." Kate stroked the rumpled orange head. "I'll have to get her into the light—but look, there are bits of her fur all over the ground. She got the worst of it, the poor old wuss."

"I saw her in the house. She must have slipped outside when we did."

"Probably." Kate nodded, racked by guilt. "I never allow her out at night. There are some huge, tough cats in this neighborhood, and she's getting too old to hold her own against them."

Flannery burst out of the house with Ellen behind her. "Mom, I heard that awful noise—where's Mehitabel? Was she fighting?"

"I've got her right here," Kate said. "She seems okay, but let's get her into the house." She led the parade to the kitchen where they spread a towel on the kitchen table and held down the wriggling animal while Flannery, who had the surest fingers, began to inspect her hide for bites. At the first probing touch on her left shoulder, Mehitabel winced and yowled.

"Oh, no!" Flannery groaned as she parted the thick orange fur to reveal a large, deep gash. The cat would need stitches, Kate calculated, her heart sinking, and an antibiotic shot—and none of it would wait until morning.

As she dialed the vet's emergency number, her eyes met Jeff's across the kitchen. There would be no more time for them to talk, she knew. Patching up Mehitabel would occupy the rest of the evening, and he would be leaving for Raleigh before dawn. Unless he phoned her, she would not speak with him again until he came to pick her up for the fund-raiser.

But he loved her, she reminded herself. He had told her so, and Jeff Parrish was not a man to speak lightly. However slim the odds, their one chance for happiness depended on her trust in that love.

She returned his gaze, willing her eyes to speak the words she could not say aloud. For now, at least, she would keep faith with him. She would hold on to the hope of what life could offer—and she would pray that, once he knew everything, he would be strong enough to understand and forgive.

Chapter Nine

The doorbell rang while Kate was threading the post of a rhinestone stud through the hole in her left earlobe. She heard the happy cadence of Flannery's feet skipping across the living room and the greeting sound of Jeff's warm baritone.

Her shaking fingers dropped the earring on the rug.

"So how did Mehitabel make out?" Jeff's question penetrated the thin wall as Kate dropped to her hands and knees, groping for the lost bauble.

"Five stitches and a shot! She'll be sore for a while, but she's getting better." Flannery's voice echoed off the walls as she bounded around the room like Bambi on speed. She would be spending the night at Ellen's, under Floss's care, and the anticipation was more than she could contain.

"Do you think my mom is beautiful?" Flannery asked, still bouncing.

"I think your mother is breathtaking," Jeff answered gallantly, "even in her Jo-Jo costume."

"Wait till you see her tonight! She looks like a fairy princess!"

"Oh? Do you think her wings will fit in my car, or should I go out and take the top off your Jeep?"

As Kate heard her daughter giggle, her groping fingers located the missing earring under the edge of the bed. She scrambled to her feet, leaned toward the glass and threaded the post through the tiny hole. Jeff sounded cheerful tonight—too cheerful, perhaps. He had not called her from Raleigh. Maybe the hospital board had rejected his design. Maybe he was joking to hide his despair.

If he had lost the contract because of her influence, she would never forgive herself.

Somehow Kate's fumbling fingers managed to fasten the earring in place. Dropping her arms, she stepped back from the mirror to survey the full effect.

She had not done too badly with her grandmother's funeral dress, she concluded. Impelled by a stroke of daring, she had cut away the entire right shoulder and arm, leaving one side bare, the other clad in a long, fitted sleeve. She had also ripped out the rusty zipper and taken in the entire body of the dress. The heavy bias-cut silk clung to her slender curves, falling to a beaded flare from knee to hem.

"You look chic and alluring, Kate Valera," she murmured, struggling to bolster her shaking confidence.

Get real, lady, her mirrored reflection mocked her, *you look like a redheaded Morticia Adams!*

With a toss of her head, Kate forced herself to turn away and stride out of the bedroom. Did she look glamorous or merely foolish? One glance at Jeff's eyes would tell her all she needed to know.

Trembling, she crossed the threshold into the living room. Jeff was standing in the middle of the carpet, his hands clasped like a nervous schoolboy's. A warm smile lit his face as he saw her. Yes, Kate reassured herself, she looked fine.

"Tell me about your meeting with the hospital board," she said, pausing halfway across the room. "I've been wishing so hard that my fingers have frozen into a permanent cross. How did it go?"

She saw him hesitate, frowning, and her heart began to ache for him. "I'll tell you exactly how it went," he said, reaching out for her. "It went...smashingly!"

His hands caught her waist and swung her off the floor in a giddy arc, around and around, while Flannery whooped her approval.

"Tell me—everything!" Kate was breathless by the time he set her down. "Were you brilliant? Did they love your design? Did they give you any trouble?"

"Yes, no and yes." He hugged her, laughing. "It was a hard sell—as I told you, they're a pretty conservative bunch, But in the end it was the design's functionality that won them over. When I showed them how the new structure could save time, money and, ultimately, lives—"

"They bought it!" Kate hugged him back. "They really, truly bought it! I love you, Mr. Jefferson Parrish!"

Jeff froze for an instant. Then, as Kate held her breath, his fingers caught the edge of her jaw, tilting her face upward, forcing her to meet his gaze. How could she ever have compared his eyes to cold steel? Kate wondered. They were quicksilver now, warm and vibrant.

"Did you mean that, Kate?" he whispered.

Kate could feel her pulse throbbing against the light touch of his fingertip. Her throat was so tight and dry that she could only nod—but she knew her answer was true. She had loved Jeff Parrish from that first impossible afternoon at Ellen's party. She had loved his maddening pride, his strength, his irascibility, his tenderness.

She would love him for as long as she lived.

"This calls for a celebration," Jeff declared, his voice husky with emotion. "I'd say we should make this a very big evening." He turned to Flannery, grinning now. "Grab your backpack, young lady. Ellen's got a big evening planned for you, too."

As Flannery vanished, skipping, down the hallway, Jeff swept Kate into his arms. "You look ravishing!" he murmured, nibbling a trail along the slope of her bare shoulder. The silky brush of his lips sent a current of desire sizzling like hot summer lightning through her body. Dizzy with anticipation, she imagined the hours ahead—coming home to the empty house, feeling Jeff's arms around her in the warm darkness, losing herself in the thrill of his unbridled kisses....

Merciful heaven, what was she thinking?

Kate shocked herself awake with a sharp mental slap. *Not this time,* she vowed. This time she was playing for keeps, and the stakes were all or nothing.

This time she would leave no room for tragic mistakes.

She would go to the fund-raiser with Jeff and do her best to be gracious and charming. Then, at the end of the evening, she would tell him everything.

She would tell him while she still had the strength to walk away.

"You make me feel reckless," he whispered, his lips moving like a slow flame against the hollow of her throat. "You make me feel as young and alive and crazy as a sixteen-year-old on prom night...."

"Shh, Flannery's coming—" Kate slipped out of his arms, smoothing her gown with nervous fingers as her daughter came bounding back into the room.

"I'm ready!" she announced, swinging her backpack. "Let's go, you beautiful people!"

"Ladies..." Jeff was grinning as he ushered them both to the car. Beside him in the darkness, Kate practiced arranging her features into a pleasant expression. She would be nice this evening if it killed her, she vowed. She would be gracious and cordial—even to Jeff's mother. She would encase her feelings in bulletproof glass that no unkind remark would penetrate. She would return verbal darts with roses. In short, she would be every inch a lady.

Whatever the emotional cost, she would make Jeff proud of her tonight.

As they walked into the yacht club, Jeff felt Kate's fingers tighten on his arm. "It'll be fine," he whispered. "You look beautiful."

And she did, he reflected. The black silk gown was perfect on her, setting off her creamy skin and flawless little dancer's body. Her subtly made-up eyes were as large and expressive as a fawn's, her hair, a flaming contrast to the starkness of her dress. Every man in the room would be covertly eyeing her tonight, envying him. As for the women... Jeff's heart sank. Most of the ladies would be polite and friendly. A few of them, however, were capable of cutting her to ribbons.

But then, Kate was a classy woman, he reminded himself. If she met any hostility, he could only hope she would be tough enough to deal with it.

The Misty Point Yacht Club, completed only last year, had been built with sliding walls to allow for gatherings of various sizes. Tonight the rooms had been opened up into one large ballroom, made grander by the presence of rainbow-colored spotlights, iridescent foil streamers, and a live jazz band imported from Atlantic City. A lavish buffet was laid out on tables at the hall's far end.

"Hang on to me," Kate whispered, clutching the sleeve

of his white dinner jacket. "I don't want to embarrass you by snatching up my skirt and bolting into the night."

"You couldn't embarrass me if you wanted to," Jeff murmured, patting her tense fingers. "I'm the proudest man here because you're with me."

The floor was already crowded with party goers—bored-looking men in tailored evening wear, women flashing their finery like tropical birds. In a far corner of the room, he spotted his mother, an imposing figure in mauve satin and pearls. Kate had seen her, too. She stiffened at his side like a small, elegant terrier, sucking in her breath before she spoke.

"Come on, let's get over and pay our respects to your mother."

"We can wait awhile if you like." Jeff's spirits darkened as he imagined the encounter between the two women. For all her well-meant courage, Kate had no idea what she could be letting herself in for. "Why don't we try the buffet?" he suggested, hoping to distract her.

"No." Kate shook her head emphatically. "I need to do this now. If I can face your mother, I can face anyone in this room." She turned and, without looking back at him, strode along the periphery of the crowded floor toward the far corner of the room. Jeff swallowed hard, then plunged after her and caught her arm.

"Kate, listen—"

"Uh-uh." She flashed him a dazzling smile. "I'm not a fool, Jeff. I know I represent everything your mother dislikes. But I refuse to spend the whole evening hiding from her. I have to do this, and if you don't want to go with me—"

"No, we're in this together, lady." He linked his arm firmly through hers. "If I can't stop you from walking into the dragon's mouth, the least I can do is come along."

His mother had caught sight of them. Jeff winced as he saw her stiffen and raise her chin in an attitude of haughty defiance. He loved Kate, and he loved his mother, but no matter who won this round, it was not going to be pretty.

It was Kate who took the lead. She glided forward, her hand outstretched and her face fixed in a gracious smile. "Mrs. Parrish, it's so nice to see you again!" she exclaimed. "I've been wanting to thank you for having my daughter over. Flannery so enjoys visiting Ellen in your home."

"Your daughter is quite welcome." Jeff's mother replied frostily, accepting Kate's hand as if someone had just offered her a slab of Limburger. "I must say it was a surprise when Lacy Anne Bodell told me you'd been appointed to our little committee. I'm sure you'll have some *very* clever ideas for raising money."

"I certainly do." Kate's pleasant expression did not waver. "In fact, if you'd care to hear about some of them now—"

"Surely they can wait for our next committee meeting. This is hardly the time or place—"

"Of course." A shadow of hurt flickered in Kate's eyes, but she swiftly masked it. Jeff's heart ached with pride and love. "I'll plan to submit my ideas in writing," she said. "That way there'll be less chance of misunderstanding."

"Yes, by all means." Jeff's mother's restless gaze scanned the crowded dance floor. "Oh, look, Jefferson, there are the Dunbars. You remember the Dunbars from Raleigh, don't you? Beauford and Phyllis and their adorable daughter, Pamela?"

Jeff nodded obligingly. He had only a dim memory of Beauford and Phyllis, but Pamela had been two years behind him in high school. A pretty girl, he recalled, but too much of a social butterfly for his taste. She had married a classmate of his, the heir to a small tobacco fortune.

"Pamela's single now, and she's spending the summer with her parents here in Misty Point," his mother was saying. "I spoke with her not fifteen minutes ago, Jefferson. She *specifically* asked about you."

Jeff felt Kate's hand quiver slightly through his sleeve, and he knew it was time for a tactful retreat. "Well, if you see her again, tell her hello for me," he said, feeling trapped and awkward. "Kate and I were just going to try the buffet table. Would you, uh, care to join us, Mother?"

"No, thank you," she huffed, causing Jeff's knees to sag with relief. "They're serving fish over there—you know I can't abide the smell of fish. But if you could bring me two of those little cucumber sandwiches on a plate, along with a glass of that pink champagne punch with a bit of ice—"

"Say no more, it's yours. We'll fill a plate, and I'll bring it right back to you." He steered Kate away with a none-too-subtle hand on her elbow. Half-bewildered, she glanced sharply up at him.

"Hey, I was doing just fine," she hissed. "How will I ever get to know your mother if you keep dragging me away from her?"

"Believe me, it's for your own safety," Jeff muttered, propelling her through the crowd. "My mother is a good woman, but when she puts her mind to it, she can make Leona Helmsley sound like Mother Teresa."

"I thought I was handling her quite well."

"Oh, you were. But trust me, she was just getting warmed up."

Kate's left eyebrow twitched in wry amusement. "I did get her message about the newly single Pamela Dunbar. Adorable, is she?"

Jeff exhaled slowly, wishing he could have taken Kate

someplace else tonight—someplace warm and intimate, with music and candles and nothing to do but gaze into her beautiful eyes and share every secret of their lives. He had wanted tonight to be special, but they had not been here fifteen minutes, and he could already see the evening unraveling thread by disastrous thread.

"Look," he sighed, "I haven't seen Pamela Dunbar since high school, and even then, she wasn't my kind of—"

"Jeff!" The willowy blonde who strode through the crowd was glowing like a Miss America finalist on the runway. "Jeff Parrish, after all these years! Why, you're as handsome as ever—I can't believe it. You remember me, don't you? It's Pamela! Pamela Dunbar!"

Pamela gushed over Jeff for a least a minute, giving Kate plenty of opportunity to study her. She was model slim with a shoulder-length mass of honey blond hair and a Riviera tan, lavishly set off by her stark white strapless gown. She was Nancy Drew, Kate mused archly—all grown up, divorced from Ned Nickerson and on the prowl for a new sleuthing partner.

"Your mother tells me you have a little girl," Pamela was saying. "She must be a charmer, especially if she takes after her daddy. I have two boys myself. They're spending the summer in Aspen with Carter—which leaves me free as a bird, in case you ever need a first mate for your sailboat. You know, I just love—"

"I'm afraid I haven't had time to get the boat out of dry dock," Jeff broke in clumsily. "Pamela, I'd like you to meet Kate Valera, one of Misty Point's best known and most talented artists."

"Oh?" Pamela's eyes swept over Kate like lasers. "Why, that's right, I remember now. My mother did mention that Jeff was dating a party clown. How amusing! You should have worn your costume tonight and given us a show!'' She threw back her head and laughed with a sensual abandon calculated to show off her lovely, golden throat.

Kate's body tensed as she steeled herself against the angry pinwheels exploding in her head. ''I think Jeff was referring to my pottery,'' she said, speaking with exquisite restraint. ''I have a piece on display tonight that's going to be auctioned for the library fund.''

''You do ceramics, too?'' Pamela's voice dripped molasses. ''Why, what a coincidence—so does my mother! She hand painted the most cunning little Nativity set last Christmas—you really should see it. In fact, why not pay her a call next week, since you have so much in common? I'd be more than happy to introduce you.''

''That's quite—all—right.'' Kate was dizzy from the effort of holding back her temper. She could sense Jeff's discomfort as he hesitated, torn between trying to smooth things over and hauling her away before she lost her head. She needed a break—now.

''Would you two excuse me for a minute?'' she murmured. ''I, uh, think I just felt something slip.''

Without a backward glance, she wheeled and made a beeline for what she hoped was the ladies' room. It was the coward's way out, she knew, but a far wiser course than holding her ground—and saying exactly what she felt like saying to Pamela Dunbar.

She reached the sanctuary of the rest room, stumbled through the door and collapsed, quivering, against the wall. By now her anger had turned inward on herself. What an idiot she was! In stalking away, she had played right into Pamela's manipulative little hands, giving her exactly what she wanted—time alone with Jeff.

Well, Pamela could have him, Kate fumed, fighting tears.

Pamela could have his mother, too. Kate Valera didn't belong here. Not in this place and not with these people. She was no match for their glamor, their polish or their diamond-edged meanness.

"Are you all right, dear?"

Kate glanced up, startled. She had thought herself alone, but now she saw that a graceful, white-haired woman of about seventy had come out of a stall and was washing her hands at one of the marble basins.

"I'm sorry," Kate stammered, "I didn't know anybody else was here."

"There's no need to apologize." The stranger wiped her bejeweled hands and extended her right one to Kate. "Olive Carling. And you, of course, would be Kate Valera. We'll be working together on the fund-raising committee."

Kate accepted the proffered handshake, surprising in its vigor. "How did you know who I was?" she asked, blinking.

Olive Carling's husky laugh matched her voice. "Why, everyone here knows who you are, dear. You've already given our complacent little milieu a much-needed jolt. I, for one, am delighted to have you among us."

"Well, you seem to be the only person who is," Kate sighed, battling the impulse to fling herself into the older woman's arms and bawl like a baby. "I feel as if I've just staggered through a Huron gauntlet, and the evening's only getting started."

"A word of advice, Kate."

"Only a word? I could use a whole thesaurus of advice!"

"Ah—you've got wit! So much the better for you!" The sapphire eyes sparkled. "Listen to me then, child, don't let those people out there intimidate you—they will, you know, if you allow it. Underneath those fancy trappings, they're all too human—and most of them are so insecure they're quaking in their handmade Italian pumps. They're the very ones who'll try to put you down—but don't stand for it, Kate. Everything you've got, you've earned, and you're every bit as good as they are!''

"That's easy enough for you to say." Kate's eyes measured Olive Carling from the top of her queenly head to the hem of her elegant silver-beaded gown. "Look at you— you're a born aristocrat! Have you ever known what it's like to be left out? Have you ever walked through a room, knowing that people were slashing you to pieces behind your back?''

"Oh, my dear child!" Olive Carling's eyes all but disappeared into crinkles of laughter. "Forty-six years ago, when I met the late Mr. Carling, I was a dancer—with the Radio City Rockettes!''

"You were what?" Kate stared at the stately figure in disbelief.

"I can still kick higher than my head, but I've learned not to do it in public. It does tend to set people on their ears." The lean, suntanned hands reached out to clasp Kate's. "You see, I've experienced all the things you're talking about. I've felt all the pain and anger you're feeling tonight, and I can't tell you how many times I wanted to turn around and walk away. But I was in love with a wonderful man, and I didn't want to lose him, so I held on, no matter how much it hurt. After a while I began to make friends—good friends, who respected me. You will, too, dear, in time, if you don't lose heart.''

Kate sighed raggedly, still torn by self-doubt. Was she strong enough to do what Olive Carling had done? Could she swallow her pride and try to make friends with the likes of Mrs. Parrish and Pamela Dunbar? "I'm sorry," she murmured, shaking her head. "I don't know what to say.''

"You don't have to say anything. Just go back out there

and show these people what you're made of. Go on, dear—
I'll be cheering for you...."

Olive Carling's firm hand was already nudging her out
the door. Kate managed to walk the rest of the distance on
her own, but as she stood once more at the edge of the
glittering crowd, the urge to turn tail and run gripped her
like a demon, and she hesitated, struggling.

Only the thought of Jeff, waiting for her, trusting her,
kept her from bolting into the night and walking the two-
mile distance home in her spike heels. Jeff had said he
loved her, Kate reminded herself, and she loved him so
much that the thought of losing him was like dying inside.
Their only chance for happiness could depend on the choice
she made tonight.

Taking time for a long, tremulous breath, she squared
her shoulders, fixed a smile on her face and forced her feet
to glide forward. She would do it, she vowed. She would
close her ears to cutting remarks and whispered innuendoes.
She would be warm, gracious and forgiving. Everything
would be all right. All she had to do was find Jeff, and—

Kate froze, panic welling as her eyes scanned the
crowded ballroom. Jeff was nowhere in sight.

She had run off and left him with Pamela Dunbar, she
remembered with a sinking heart. But she had been gone
only a few minutes. Surely Jeff wouldn't—he couldn't—

Relief washed over her as she caught sight of Pamela
dancing with a bespectacled stranger. She was being foolish, Kate lectured herself. Jeff had probably just ducked
into the men's room. Any minute, now, he would come
wandering out and find her.

She hovered along the periphery of the dance floor, trying not to look agitated as the seconds ticked past. Only as
she was caving in to despair did she remember that he had
promised to bring his mother a plate from the buffet table.

Yes—now things were beginning to make more sense. Moving at a deliberately casual pace, she strolled toward the table. No Jeff—but then, he had probably gone to find his mother. She would no doubt find them together.

Once more Kate's eyes scanned the ballroom, but there was no sign of the imposing Mrs. Parrish anywhere. Unsure of what to do next, she picked up a goblet of punch from the table, balanced it between her hands and sauntered on around the far side of the ballroom.

It was only by chance that she heard their muffled voices—Jeff's low and taut, his mother's shrill with indignation. But even when she stood perfectly still and strained her ears, Kate could only guess at what they were saying. For the first few seconds, in fact, she was not even sure where the voices were coming from. Then she noticed the half-open doorway leading out onto the verandah.

A bitter lump rose in her throat as she set the glass down on an empty table and slipped out into the night. It didn't take a Ph.D. to conclude that Jeff and his mother were arguing, or to guess what that argument was about. Wisdom whispered that she should stay clear of it—turn around, walk away and pretend she hadn't heard. But a more compelling voice drove her through the foggy darkness, along the brass railing toward the spot where she could see them now, facing each other in a circle of lamplight.

Neither Jeff nor his mother had seen her, but Kate could hear them distinctly now. She froze in the shadow of a tall, potted hibiscus, her stomach clenching in a knot of despair as she listened.

"Mother, I don't need to hear this now." Jeff's voice rasped with frustration and ill-bridled anger.

"Then when will you hear it?" his mother snapped. "After it's too late? After you've let this woman destroy your life?"

"Kate doesn't have a destructive bone in her body. She's *renewed* my life. I've never been happier—can't you see that?"

"What I see is your blindness, Jefferson. When you won't even let me tell you what I learned—"

"That's enough." Jeff turned to go, but she caught his sleeve, jerking him back toward her. Behind them, the lights of the marina glowed through the fog, casting rippled reflections on the black water.

"If you'd listen for once—"

"No, you heard me the first time. If there's something I should know about Kate's past, I want to hear it from her, not from you or anybody else." He took a step backward, his eyes glinting like silver ice in the lamplight. "I respect you, Mother, and I appreciate all you've done for Ellen and me. But when I think about your hiring that sleazy private eye to investigate the woman I love, I could—"

"No!" The cry leapt from Kate's throat. She saw them turn as she stepped out of the shadows and walked swiftly toward them. "I won't stand for this," she said. "Jeff, I won't have you fighting with your own mother—not because of me."

"Then you tell him." Mrs. Parrish loomed through the nighttime mist like the iceberg that sank the *Titanic*. "Tell him the truth—that you were never married, that your daughter is an illegitimate—"

"Don't you dare!" Kate lashed out as her temper flamed like a match dropped in gasoline. "I don't care who you think you are, Mrs. Parrish, *nobody* uses that word to describe my daughter. Flannery was the one pure, innocent party—"

"You don't have to put yourself through this, Kate." Jeff's voice was low and flat, masking his emotions. "Come on, I'll take you inside. We can talk later."

"No, it has to be now." Kate forced herself to speak calmly. "I meant to tell you the truth all along. I wanted to tell you at my house the other night—but the cat got hurt, and it didn't happen. So I planned to tell you tonight, on the way home. Unfortunately your mother beat me to it."

"My mother isn't part of this," Jeff said.

"She is now." Kate glanced at Mrs. Parrish, who appeared to be frozen in a state of shocked silence. "Sit down, both of you. I'll tell you the whole story, and then I'll be leaving."

"Kate..." Jeff made a move toward her, but she stopped him with a warning flash of her eyes. If she did not speak now, when would she have the courage again?

"It was the summer after my grandfather died..." She willed her voice not to tremble as they settled into listening—Mrs. Parrish on the edge of a nearby deck chair, and Jeff still on his feet, too restless to sit. "I had just finished high school, and I was planning to sell the house to pay for college. My head was full of plans—the last thing I expected was to fall in love."

As Kate paused for breath, her eyes flickered to Jeff's impassive face. *Say something,* she pleaded silently. *Say you understand, or that you love me, or even that you hate me. Just don't look at me like that!*

Jeff's lips parted, but he did not speak. Kate glanced down at her hands, steeled herself and plunged ahead with her story.

"I won't tell you his name, but you'd recognize the family. Maybe you even know them. Maybe you even know *him,* but that doesn't matter anymore. He was vacationing here, with his parents. We met on the beach. He was...what can I say? Beautiful? Brilliant? I loved him with all the power of my innocent young heart. I believed every pretty lie he told me—and whatever he wanted, I willingly gave.

"His parents looked the other way. They knew, you see, that I was only a harmless summer fling. But not me—in my foolish naiveté, I was already weaving dreams of our future together. I imagined our home, our children—I even had their names picked out. The night he told me it was over—I couldn't believe it at first. I thought he was teasing me—"

A soft moan escaped Jeff's lips. Kate heard it, but she could not look at him. If she met his eyes, she knew she would never be able to finish her story.

"When I refused to accept the end of the relationship, he told me the truth—that he'd been engaged for the past year to a girl he'd known all his life. His fiancée had decided to spend the summer trousseau-shopping in Europe, and he...he was bored, he told me. He'd decided he was entitled to one last fling before the wedding."

Mrs. Parrish's breath caught, but she said nothing—which was just as well. Even Jeff's silence was preferable to words, Kate told herself. She didn't care about their sympathy, or even their understanding. All she wanted was to set the record straight and leave with what little remained of her dignity.

"You can guess the rest of the story," she said. "I never saw him again. He was married five weeks later, and shortly after that, I learned that Flannery was on the way—I never told him. I gave up my college plans and kept the house. I wanted to raise my child in the home where I'd been raised—with so much love...." Kate's voice broke as her emotions began to crumble. She blinked back tears, fighting for self-control.

"Kate, it's all right," Jeff said, taking a tentative step

toward her. "No one could blame you—you were young and innocent, you made a mistake—"

"No!" Kate's mother instincts flared to sudden ferocity. "That's what you need to understand—both of you. It *wasn't* a mistake. Flannery was a gift and a blessing—that child has been the pride and joy of my whole life! I have no regrets! Not a single one!"

Silence hung on the air like smoke after a gunshot. Several seconds passed before Mrs. Parrish stirred and spoke.

"Well!" she sniffed. "All I can say is, things have certainly changed since I was a girl! No regrets, indeed!" She shivered, hugging her arms. "It's getting chilly out here, and I just heard a mosquito—are you quite finished?"

"Almost." Kate squared her shoulders, the worst of her fears gone now that the confession was out. But even as she spoke, she could feel her heart contract.

"Jeff," she said softly, "this is for you, but your mother needs to hear it, too." She glanced from the man she loved to his proud, stubborn mother, feeling as if she were about to jump off a precipice. The words she had to say would be more difficult than any she had ever spoken.

"I almost bought the dream this time," she said. "For a little while, I dared to imagine that Flannery and I might fit into your lives. But it seems I haven't learned all that much in ten years. It was just another illusion. I apologize for wanting it so badly that I let it pull me in, exactly the way I did the first time."

"It's not the same, Kate!" Jeff's voice was hoarse with emotion. "You know it isn't the same. I love you, and I'd never do what he did—"

"You wouldn't have to," she said softly, aching with love for him. "Don't you see that? If I were to stay, it would drive a wedge right down the middle of your family. My daughter and I would always be the outsiders, the interlopers, the spoilers—you'd come to resent that after a while, and for me, that would be ten times worse than not having you at all.''

"Dammit, Kate, I can't just let you go like this—"

"No," she said gently, cutting off his words before they could shatter her resolve. "I have to leave now, while I'm still able. Don't make this ugly by coming after me, Jeff. I know a couple of the servers—one of them can run me home on her break. Flannery will take it hard, but maybe it's time she learned that not all fairy tales come true—"

"This is the last time I'm asking!" Jeff's mother huffed, pulling herself to her feet. "Are you quite finished?"

"Yes, except for one thing," Kate declared, facing her squarely, head held high. "I've spent most of my life in awe of you so-called summer people—your big houses, your expensive clothes and flashy cars—but that's about to change. I don't want my daughter growing up the way I did, feeling like a second-class citizen of Misty Point because she lives here year-round. It's up to me to set an example for her, and the first thing I'm going to do is serve on your fund-raising committee. I'll be at your planning luncheon on Wednesday with a whole portfolio of ideas, and if that bothers you, you can always cancel your—"

"Don't underestimate me, Miss Valera. I plan to be there, too. We'll all be waiting for you to prove your worth."

Kate met the older woman's strong, gray eyes—so like Jeff's—and caught the spark of challenge in them. It was the challenge of equal to equal. "I'll do my best," she answered quietly. "And now, if you'll excuse me—"

"Kate, we can work this out." Jeff's shadowed face revealed nothing, but the anguish in his voice tore at her heart. "You don't have to do this."

"Yes, I do." Kate forced herself to back away from him. "If ever there was anything I had to do, it's this. Goodbye, Jeff."

Faster than she could think, or even breathe, she turned away and walked swiftly toward the kitchen.

Chapter Ten

Kate pulled the Jeep into the darkness of the Parrish driveway and tapped the horn. Her fingers drummed an anguished tattoo on the steering wheel as she waited for Flannery to emerge from the house.

The assistant chef at the yacht club had dropped her off
at home. From there she had telephoned Flannery and told
her to gather up her things and be ready to leave. "We'll
talk after I pick you up," she'd hedged when her daughter
had demanded to know what was going on. "Hurry, now."

Feeling like the driver of a getaway car, she glanced
anxiously back over her shoulder. She had feared that Jeff
might be waiting when she came to get Flannery, but there
was no sign of him. He'd probably stayed at the party,
where Pamela Dunbar was no doubt enjoying a field day.
And that was just as well, Kate reminded herself bitterly.
When she'd told him the relationship was over, she had
meant every word.

Light flooded the porch as the front door opened. Floss
waved discreetly as Flannery's lean shadow flitted down

the steps toward the Jeep. Kate leaned across the seat and opened the door for her daughter.

"Mom, what's the matter?" Flannery demanded as she piled inside and flung her backpack into the rear seat. "You said I could stay all night! We were having fun! This isn't fair!"

"No, sweetheart, it isn't fair." Heartsick, Kate ground the gears as she shifted the Jeep into Reverse and backed down the driveway. "It's especially not fair to you and Ellen, but it can't be helped. Fasten your seat belt."

"What happened? Did you have a fight?"

"Not exactly. Jeff and I just...decided not to see each other anymore, that's all." Kate swung the vehicle onto the main road, tires spattering gravel.

"But it's not supposed to happen that way!" Flannery wailed. "He was going to ask you to marry him!"

Kate's throat tightened into a painful knot. "Don't go making things up, young lady," she muttered. "I feel rotten enough as it is."

"I'm not making it up—it's true! Ellen heard him telling her grandma, and she told me! It was our big secret—we were going to be real sisters! Why did you have to go and spoil it?" She slumped in the seat, her lower lip thrust outward like the spout on an old-fashioned cream pitcher.

Kate sighed as she eased off on the gas and peered through the swirling fog. "I didn't have any choice except to spoil it, honey," she said. "I've known all along it would never work out. Now the ball is over, the spell is broken, and it's time for the Little Mermaid to go back to the sea."

"Are you saying you broke up with Ellen's dad because the Parrishes are rich and we aren't? Mom, that's really dumb!"

"Is it?" Kate swallowed the lump in her throat.

"It doesn't matter to Ellen or to me! Why should it matter to a bunch of stupid grown-ups?"

"That's enough, Flannery. I've got a headache." Kate dimmed her headlights for a passing car and realized it was Jeff's BMW. Her heart jumped, then dropped leadenly as the red taillights vanished in her rearview mirror without slowing down.

Maybe he hadn't seen her—but then, she hadn't wanted him to see her, Kate reminded herself. Besides, he was probably with Pamela or with his mother. What difference did it make? He was just a summer man, and the relationship was over. If she ever saw him again, it would only be by accident.

He was going to ask you to marry him! Flannery's words sang in her head, mocking her crumbled hopes. Even if Jeff had been crazy enough to ask her—and even if she had been foolhardy enough to accept—their marriage would have been a disaster, Kate reminded herself. True, Olive Carling had made a similar situation work. But then, Kate would lay odds that Olive Carling hadn't had to deal with the likes of Mrs. Parrish as a mother-in-law.

Kate drove the rest of the way home in silent misery, feeling empty and cold and lost. She had done the right thing, she told herself again and again. She had ended the game before things got ugly and hurtful. One day she would be glad of it. But right now she could feel her whole world dissolving like a sand castle at high tide.

She glanced at her mournful little daughter, knowing it would be a long time before Flannery forgave her—and knowing it would be much, much longer before Kate Valera dared to reach out and love a man again.

Jeff stared morosely into the dregs of his coffee and tried, for perhaps the twentieth time that day, to focus his attention on his work. The hospital board would be reviewing the plans again tomorrow, and there was still much to be done. But somehow, without Kate to cheer him on, his enthusiasm for the project was flagging. Until this week, he would never have believed he could need anyone so much.

The last four days had passed as painfully as a session on the rack. Scarcely an hour had gone by when he had not battled the temptation to pick up the phone and dial her number. Half a dozen times he had even reached for the receiver, only to stop cold. It had been Kate's decision to end the relationship. Pride and caution argued that it was not his place to try and change her mind.

Pamela Dunbar had called twice with sailing and picnic invitations. He had put her off, using the hospital plans as an excuse. A few weeks ago he might have been interested. But now—

"Jefferson!" His mother's voice echoed up the stairs as the front door clicked shut. She had been at her weekly committee luncheon much of the afternoon and would no doubt be eager to give him a full report—especially if that report included Kate.

"Up here." Bracing himself for the ordeal, he walked out onto the landing and started down the stairs. It would be less painful to meet her on neutral ground than wait for her to invade his studio, he reasoned. Things had been strained between them for the past few days, but she *was* his mother and he owed her, at least, a modicum of courtesy.

"So how did we do the other night?" he asked her, striving to be pleasant. "Did the party and the auction make enough money to put the new library over the top?"

"Almost," she huffed, lowering her rigidly corseted body to the edge of a chair and fanning her damp chest with a copy of *Town and Country*. "The fund is still a few thousand dollars short, but we're planning another event for the twenty-sixth—a town fair and carnival to honor the one-hundredth anniversary of the founding of Misty Point. With luck, that will bring us to our goal. Oh—incidently, the whole thing was your Miss Valera's idea."

"She's hardly *my* Miss Valera," Jeff countered, grateful, in spite of everything, that at least his mother had stopped calling Kate "that Jo-Jo woman." "But it's not a bad idea. I confess I had no idea the town had a centennial coming up."

"Neither did anyone else on the committee. But she stood up as bold as a strumpet and presented her plan, and when Olive Carling backed her, the rest of us had no choice except to vote it in. You know how pushy Olive can be when she sets her mind on something—it comes of her common breeding, I suppose. The only one who balked was Lacy Anne Bodell."

"Oh?" Jeff studied the stonework in the fireplace, feigning a disinterest he did not feel. "So what happened?"

"Lacy Anne did come around—but only after your Miss Valera agreed to do her clown act for the children at the carnival."

"Kate didn't want to?"

"Mercy, no! She made it very clear that she wanted to appear at the carnival as an artist and a member of the committee. But Lacy Anne went into one of her little black pouts—you know how she can be, Jefferson—and so, to keep the peace—"

"Kate caved in and agreed to do Jo-Jo." Jeff bit back the urge to swear under his breath. He knew how much pride and courage it had cost Kate to stand before the committee and present her plan. At least they could have treated her with the respect she deserved, instead of relegating her to a role that set her apart and left her powerless.

"Actually, I agreed with Lacy Anne," his mother was saying. "The children will need some entertainment, and after all, the woman *is* a party clown—"

"Kate is a fine artist and a sensitive person," Jeff interjected, startled by his own anger, "and if you ask me, your precious committee gave her an uncalled-for slap in the face!"

"Jefferson!" The magazine dropped from her hand, slithered over her knees and fell to the floor. "What's gotten into you the past few days? You haven't been yourself at all!"

"No, I don't suppose I have." Jeff retrieved the magazine from the floor. He took his time placing it back on the coffee table, thinking and wondering as he moved.

"Tell me something," he said, "were you and Father happy together?"

"What kind of a question is that?" she snapped, blinking at him.

"A question I have to ask," Jeff replied gently. "Maybe the answer will help me understand some things better—like myself."

She stared out the window, avoiding his eyes. "Your father was an excellent provider. He was a dutiful husband and father—"

"But were you happy, Mother? Was he?"

"You're being cruel, Jefferson."

"Only because I need to know."

She exhaled wearily, her shoulders sagging. "Your father didn't know how to be happy. He wasn't raised that way. He only knew rules—how to make them, how to impose them, what to do if they were broken—"

"What about you?"

"I was...eighteen when I married, too young to know my own mind. I'd been raised to be a good, submissive wife, so I allowed my husband to mold me to his way of thinking. I allowed him to mold your sister Joanna and you—"

"Joanna is a lonely, driven workaholic." Jeff sank onto an ottoman, weak with dismay. "And look at me! I tried to control Meredith the same way Father controlled us all— it seemed so natural. I could never figure out why she left me—until now!"

"Your wife was too headstrong for her own good!" Jeff's mother stood up and brushed the creases out of her skirt. "Now, Ellen is different. She's very much the sort of child you were, quiet and thoughtful and obedient. All she needs is the kind of mother who'll set her a good ex-ample—and frankly, Jefferson, it's high time you found her one."

She marched upstairs to change her dress, leaving Jeff alone. For the space of a long breath he sat staring out the window at the clouds, uncertain whether to laugh or weep. Why hadn't he seen it before? His father's rigid, rule-bound code had darkened almost every life it touched—his own, his mother's, his sister's, Meredith's and even Ellen's. For generation after generation it had weighed upon his family, exacting its bitter toll from every member.

Until Kate Valera.

It had taken Kate—spirited, unconventional Kate—to jar him out of his lethargy and show him what it meant to be alive. It had taken Kate, and her lively little daughter, to open Ellen to the world of imagination and laughter that was part of every child's birthright. It had taken Kate to teach him how to love.

Kate had made all the difference in his life. And he had let her go.

Jeff sprang to his feet, propelled by an urgency that would not let him rest. It wasn't too late—it couldn't be too late. He could call her—make up some excuse to see her again. Surely, once he got his arms around her, she would see that they were meant to be together.

He would get her back, Jeff vowed, this time for keeps. But first he had to find a way past the barrier of Kate's stubborn pride. For that, it would help to have an ally. Kate had been deeply hurt that night at the yacht club, and she might well refuse to see him—but how could she refuse his daughter?

"Ellen?" Taking the stairs two at a time, he raced up to her bedroom, where he'd seen her drawing pictures earlier that afternoon. "Hey, honey, how would you like to help out a desperate man?"

The question echoed off the daintily flowered walls and faded into unanswered silence. Ellen was not there.

Jeff paused in the doorway, wondering whether she might have gone down to the kitchen for a snack. Only as he turned away did he notice the hand-written note pinned to her pillow. Worried now, he strode across the room and snatched it up. His heart contracted in sudden fear as he read the carefully-penned message.

Dear Daddy and Grandma,
Flannery and I want to be sisters, but you grown-ups say we can't, so we have gone off together to be mermaids. Goodbye forever.

Love,
Ellen

Kate swung the Jeep into her own driveway, switched off the ignition and sank back into the seat with a weary sigh. She had survived the committee luncheon, but the experience had been like facing a circle of woman-eating tigers, armed with nothing but a chair and a toy whip. The afternoon had left her drained, exhausted and quivering with frustration.

For a time she had almost thought she could win. Olive Carling's support had helped swing the other members behind her plan for the town fair. Some of the women, in fact, had become quite enthusiastic. Even Mrs. Parrish had been civil in her cold, distant way. Kate had begun to relax a little. Then Lacy Anne Bodell had unsheathed her claws and delivered a lightning-quick, underhanded belly swipe.

"Well," she'd simpered, "I'm not sure what kind of carnival we can put together on two weeks' notice, but at least we know we'll have a clown. That's you, of course, Jo-Jo."

The afternoon had gone sour at that point—especially when Kate faced the snarling assemblage and announced that she didn't *want* to do her clown act—that she preferred to set up her pottery wheel and demonstrate her craft. The congressman's wife had countered with a display of pique that would have put a two-year-old to shame. After that—

But why relive the torture all over again? Kate lashed herself as she piled out of the Jeep and slammed the door. She had caved in and agreed to do Jo-Jo, and that was that. If she didn't like the idea, she had no one to blame but herself.

From inside the house, the sudden ringing of the phone scattered her thoughts. Kate fumbled with her key, hurrying, but not too much. Flannery had stayed home that afternoon, pleading a stomachache. Any second now she would hear the sound and pick up the receiver.

But the phone was still shrilling when Kate opened the

door. Sprinting across the living room, she caught it just before the answering machine clicked on.

"Kate?" Jeff's voice stopped her heart.

"What—is it?" she asked, caught off balance. After the awful scene at the yacht club, she had prayed he wouldn't call her. Then, for three sleepless nights, she had prayed he would. Now that he had...

"I'm looking for Ellen," he said, plummeting her back to reality. "She's not over there, is she?"

"I don't think so," Kate muttered, still reeling. "I just got home."

"Is Flannery there?" The strain in his voice sobered her like a dash of cold water.

"She's supposed to be. Hang on, I'll check." Kate flew down the hall to her daughter's bedroom. No Flannery. There was only a folded page from the mermaid notebook tucked under the leg of Flannery's hug-worn teddy bear. Snatching it up, she raced back to the phone.

"Jeff—she's gone. She left a note—it says—"

"I know what it says. Ellen left one, too."

"Those little monkeys..." Kate's breath caught in sudden fear. "They could be in danger! We've got to find them—stop them—"

"Where would they go to be mermaids?"

Kate's mind scrambled, groping for answers. Then, suddenly, she knew. "The rock—"

"The one where we found them before—"

"Yes—hurry!" Kate was already kicking off her high-heeled pumps. "Don't wait for me! I'll meet you there!"

He hung up without saying goodbye. Kate sprinted down the hall to her room, flung off her linen suit and yanked on rumpled shorts, a clay-spattered T-shirt and rubber sandals. Seconds later, she was in the Jeep again, flying down the highway.

It was her own fault, she lashed herself as she swung, squealing rubber, onto the beach road. In her stubborn pride, she'd concluded that breaking things off with Jeff was the best thing for herself and her daughter—but she hadn't taken Flannery's feelings, or Ellen's, into account. If the girls had done something reckless, she would never forgive herself.

She drove to the spot where the road dissolved in sand at the foot of the dunes. Heart pounding, she sprang out of the Jeep and began to scramble up the sandy leeward slope. What if Flannery and Ellen had gone into the treacherous water? What if they were really trying to become mermaids?

Please, Kate prayed silently. *Please let them be all right!*

Her foot slipped on the sand. She went down, clawing like a wildcat, then clambered to her feet again. Maybe Jeff had already found the girls. His house was not far from the rocky point. Running, he could make it there in a few minutes.

But what if he'd arrived too late? What if their daughters weren't there? What then?

Panting, Kate reached the top of the dune. Her knees went wobbly with relief as she spotted three figures on the beach below—Jeff, Ellen and Flannery standing at the edge of the surf. The girls were safe. Everything was all right.

Wild with clashing emotions, she alternately ran, slid and tumbled down the dune. The trio on the beach watched her, all of them strangely quiet as she collapsed in the river of sand she had dislodged on her way. Jeff's face was grim, but his eyes twinkled mysteriously as he reached down to assist her.

"It seems we have a conspiracy here," he said.

"We have a *what?*" Kate gripped his strong, brown hand and pulled herself to her feet.

"To make a long story short, we've been set up."

"Don't be mad, Mom," Flannery broke in. "Ellen and I weren't really going to be mermaids. We only ran away so you two would come looking for us."

"We thought that if you could see each other and talk, you might decide to get back together," said Ellen.

Shaken, Kate sank back onto the sand. "You had me so scared," she muttered, wagging an indignant finger at her daughter. "If you ever, ever pull a stunt like this again—"

"We won't," Flannery said. "And now Ellen and I will go sit in the Jeep so you two can talk and hug and kiss."

"We won't go anywhere else, we promise," Ellen added solemnly.

Grinning at each other, the two small conspirators joined hands and started up the dune. "Wait!" Kate sputtered. "You can't just—"

"Let them go." Jeff had moved behind her, his hands on her shoulders firmly compelling. "There's no harm done. After all, maybe we do need to talk. And hug. And kiss."

Kate moaned as his fingers worked the tension out of her tight shoulder muscles. "Jeff, I'm not ready for this," she said. "I don't know if I'll ever be ready."

"Do you love me, Kate?" he asked gently. "Be honest."

"Yes," she whispered, knowing, for all her fears, that it was true. "But sometimes love isn't enough. No one knows that better than I do."

"So what would make it enough? What would it take for your stubborn little heart to give us a real chance?"

Kate's throat jerked as a freshet of tears scalded her eyes. Jeff was laying it all on the line for her—his pride, his love and his future. If she let her fears push him away now, she knew she would lose him forever.

"I—need time first," she said, staring down at her hands, afraid to grasp something so precious. "I need some time without pressure, to think, to know my own mind."

"You can have all the time you need, Kate," he said. "For starters, I need to go back to Raleigh for a couple of weeks to work on the plans with the hospital board. Ellen's going with me to give my mother a rest, so we'll both be out of your hair until the twenty-sixth."

"That's the day of the town carnival." Kate managed a bitter chuckle. "You'll be back here just in time to see my Jo-Jo act."

"You'll make a lovely Jo-Jo," he said, "but that's not what we were talking about. What else would you need to make this work?"

"What else?" Kate closed her eyes, probing the raw darkness of her own emotions. Unless she could speak from her heart in total honesty, she knew, there was no hope for them. "I need to know that you and I can share the same world as equals," she said. "I need to know that whatever happens, whatever I say or do, you won't be ashamed of me."

"I could never be ashamed of you, you little dunce." He bent down and brushed a light kiss across her curls.

"That's not what I'm saying." She glanced up at him, only to be dizzied by the love in his eyes. "I've tried to fit into your life, your world—but every time I make an effort, I manage to come out bruised and bleeding and humiliated." Her hand reached up to clasp his, seeking strength and reassurance. "Don't you see how impossible it is? I can't become a different person, Jeff. I'm me—Kate Valera, living in a run-down beach house and scratching for every cent. I'm a struggling artist. I'm an off-season waitress at the Pancake Palace. I'm the unwed mother of a fantastic little girl. I'm Jo-Jo, the second-rate party clown!"

"I know what you are." His hand tightened hard around hers. "You're strong and brave and passionate and delightful. You're the woman I love, Kate."

"But is that enough for you?" The question tore itself like an uprooted thornbush from the depths of Kate's fear. "Can you love and accept me as I am, even when I fall on my silly face and embarrass you half to death in front of your mother and your blue-blooded friends? Can you value my own world for what it is—and can you willingly and lovingly become part of it? That's what I have to know, Jeff, before we can move on to whatever comes next. That's the one thing I need most of all!"

Drained by her own outburst, she stared down at the rumpled, white sand. For a long moment Jeff's fingers lay still on her shoulder. Then she felt him tugging her to her feet and turning her gently to face him.

"I think it's time for one of those hugs your daughter mentioned," he muttered, gathering her close.

Kate surrendered willingly, her arms sliding around his rib cage, pulling him tightly against her. "I'm sorry," she whispered into the broad, hard warmth of his chest. "That's a pretty tall order I just gave you. If it's more than you can handle, I need to know."

"You crazy little lady." His lips grazed her hair, her temple, her damp forehead. "I could stand here and spout pretty words till the moon came up, and it still wouldn't be enough to convince you, would it?"

"I—don't know." Kate quivered in his arms, knowing that if she lost him now her whole world would shatter like the tiny crystal unicorn he had dropped on her floor.

"You asked for time," he said. "Give me some time, too, Kate. I'll find a way to *show* you this can work."

"Show me? I'm not sure I understand. How..." She pulled back slightly, looking up at him.

"Leave that to me," he murmured huskily, bending close. "Incidentally, your daughter also mentioned kissing. We wouldn't want to go back to the Jeep having disappointed her, would we?"

With a little half sob, Kate melted back into his embrace.

"So, are you and Kate going to get married or not?"

Ellen's question did not come as a surprise, but its timing startled Jeff. They had been driving toward Raleigh since dawn, and for the past two hours she had been sound asleep, nestled in the back seat beneath her pink bunny blanket. Now, suddenly, she was wide awake, grilling him like an FBI interrogator.

"Well, are you?" she demanded when he did not answer right away.

"You must be getting hungry," he said, half-teasingly. "How would you like to stop for breakfast in the next town?"

"Daddy! Will you just answer my question?"

Jeff sighed. "I wish I could, honey, but that's up to Kate. She says she needs time to think."

Ellen's little huff of exasperation reminded Jeff of his mother's. "What is there to think about? Do you and Kate love each other?"

"Uh-huh."

"Do you want to sleep together and have babies?"

"I—uh—guess that's part of it." Jeff wondered whether he was blushing.

"Well, then you really need to get married, Daddy, and that's that."

Jeff managed to chuckle. "You make it sound so simple," he said, easing up on the gas pedal as the car approached an off ramp.

"It *is* simple. Why does Kate need to think about it?"

Jeff sighed. "Kate's worried about how people will treat her—people like your grandmother and Mrs. Bodell."

"Why? She doesn't have to marry *them.*"

"I see a restaurant down there," said Jeff, signaling a right turn. "What would you like for breakfast? Waffles?"

"French toast with blueberries." Ellen bounced up and down in the rearview mirror. "Why should Kate care about other people? She'll have you and me and Flannery. We'll be a family. Oh, please make her say yes, Daddy!"

"I'm certainly working on it." And he had been, Jeff mused wearily. All night and all morning he had thought about little else except how to give Kate what she wanted—tangible proof that she would always be loved and accepted. He had racked his brain, examined and rejected a dozen different plans. Nothing felt right.

"Just think," Ellen was saying, "if Kate was my mom, she could read me stories every night. And she could show me how to make pots, too. Maybe if I asked her, she'd even teach me to be a clown. Flannery and I could get costumes and make up our own clown act! Wouldn't that be cool?"

"Very cool," Jeff murmured in response; and suddenly his pulse leapt as an idea clicked into place—an idea so farfetched and preposterous that it almost made him laugh out loud. The plan was crazy, he lectured himself. Worse, it was a gamble. If it fell flat, Kate would never forgive him.

All the same, the more he thought about it, the more he realized it was the answer he'd been searching for. It had to be—and he had to make it work.

"You look funny," Ellen said. "Are you all right, Daddy?"

Jeff pulled up in front of the restaurant and switched off the engine. "Never better," he said. "But I'm going to need your help with a surprise I'm planning for Kate. Come on inside, and we'll talk about it over blueberry waffles.''

Kate leaned close to the finger-smudged rest room mirror to recheck the makeup she'd applied so carefully at home. Her purple wig was combed, fluffed and firmly in place. Her tie-dyed costume was freshly washed and ironed, her huge, floppy shoes laced and tied in double knots. For better or for worse, Jo-Jo the Clown was ready to go to work.

Outside in the square, the Misty Point Centennial Carnival was already in full swing. Summer residents and year-rounders alike had turned out in force to enjoy the craft boutiques, food booths, games and kiddie rides. Now it was time for the entertainment to start.

Kate drank deeply from the water bottle in her bag and prepared herself for an exhausting afternoon. She would be giving three performances on the makeshift stage, and in between she would be expected to roam the square and mingle with the crowds, stopping here and there to make and sell her balloon animals. It was all for the new children's library, she reminded herself. Even so, the last thing she felt like today was being a clown.

She took a deep breath, fixed a comic smile on her face and tried to forget that she had not heard from Jeff in more than two weeks. True, they had agreed not to talk until he returned from Raleigh—that in response to her request for time to think. But that had been a mistake. As the days dragged lifelessly past, she had only grown more miserable. With every waking moment, she had ached to pick up the phone and hear the sound of Jeff's voice.

What an idiot she'd been—pleading for more time, demanding proof of his unconditional love! What was wrong with her? Why had she been so fearful, so hesitant to open herself to the precious gift of a man's heart?

What if she had expected too much? What if she had already lost him?

"Two minutes, Jo-Jo!" Lacy Anne Bodell, chic and immaculate in an ivory pantsuit, popped her freshly coiffed head into the rest room. "Do you have your music tape, dear? I'll give it to the sound man for you."

"Thanks, but he already has it." Kate focused on restoring a smudged lipline with her finger. "I'll be there in a second."

"Break a leg!" Lacy Anne waved and vanished, trailing a fragrant cloud of Giorgio in her wake.

Kate turned away from the mirror with a sigh. In an effort to buoy her own spirits, she broke into the little hip-hop dance that usually opened her act. It did not help. She shuffled across the grass to the back of the stage feeling blue and utterly alone. Even Flannery had deserted her, pleading one of her mysterious stomachaches. It was going to be a very long afternoon.

In the wings, she scooted her duffel into position and nodded to the teenaged boy who was running the sound system. The tape clicked on, and as the rollicking circus theme blared from the speakers, Kate pranced onto the stage.

She warmed up the crowd with a few heel clicks, a trio of spins, and her first trick—pulling a string of silk scarves out of her sleeve. Next it was time for her juggling act. Kate was just reaching into her pocket for the fluorescent balls when it happened.

Two small clowns in matching harlequin costumes came somersaulting up the aisle and jumped, giggling, onto the stage. Seizing Kate's hands, they skipped around and around with her in a giddy circle.

"Flannery—Ellen!" she gasped, struggling to make the dance look planned. "What on earth is going on?"

"Surprise, Mom!" Flannery grinned up at her through a layer of clown-white makeup. "Jo-Jo just became an ensemble!"

But the surprise was not over. A howl of laughter went up from the audience as a tall, husky clown in a red polka-dot tramp costume bumbled out of the wings, tripped over the duffel bag and executed a spectacular pratfall onto the stage.

Kate stared at him, open-mouthed, as he scrambled to his feet. Before she had time to recover her wits, he had crossed the distance between them and, with one powerful motion, swept her off her feet, into his arms.

Gray eyes, steely with tenderness beneath bushy fake eyebrows, gazed straight into her soul.

"Jeff!" she whispered, dumbfounded. "What do you think you're doing? Everybody's staring at us—put me down!"

"Not until you listen to me." His voice was a low rasp. "I love you, Kate Valera. I want a life together—you and me and our girls, and if this is what it takes to convince you we belong together..."

Kate's tears surged like a fountain. They pooled in her eyes, spilling over the lids to float down her greasepainted cheeks. She had asked for proof of Jeff's love, but never in her wildest dreams had she imagined that staid, dignified Jefferson Parrish III would go this far to win her.

"You—crazy fool!" she sputtered, overcome with emotion. "I don't know what to say!"

"Just one word. What'll it be, lady?"

"Yes!" Kate flung her arms around his neck and kissed him, heedless of the cheering, clapping crowd, heedless of the makeup that would be a smeared mess when they finally broke apart.

As he lowered her feet gently to the stage, Flannery and

Ellen danced around them, shouting and skipping, then stopping to hug and be hugged. People would be talking about them for years to come, Kate realized, but she no longer cared. The four of them together—yes, it felt right and natural and perfect.

It felt like family.

Epilogue

Jefferson Parrish IV, scarcely an hour old, lay snuggled in a fleecy blue blanket, gazing up at his family.

"Look—he's got my hair!" Flannery whispered, brushing a fingertip over the soft reddish fuzz.

"And he's got my eyes!" Ellen's voice was hushed with childish wonder.

"He's got little pieces of us all," Jeff said. "That's what makes him so special. He belongs to all of us."

"And we belong to each other." Kate lay back on the pillows with a sigh of weary bliss. Her life with Jeff and the girls had been wonderful from the start. Now it was perfect.

They had remodeled the old Parrish summer cottage into a permanent home, with an office for Jeff adjoining Kate's well-equipped pottery studio. Jeff's mother, of course, had returned to Raleigh. Kate's relationship with her mother-in-law was still prickly at best, but the distance made things easier.

Jo-Jo had hung up her clown shoes after the memorable

town carnival, and Kate no longer had time to miss her old clown self. For the past eighteen months she had been a full-time artist and mother. Now her work was showing in galleries as far away as Atlantic City and Baltimore. Next year it would be New York, she had vowed—but right now, as she lay enfolded in a warm circle of love, nothing seemed as important as her family.

A nurse bustled quietly into the room and slipped a note into Jeff's hand. His face fell as he read it.

"So much for peace and quiet," he muttered. "Mother's on her way. She'll be here in about twenty minutes. Want me to try and stall her?"

Kate skimmed a kiss across her son's tiny button nose. "No," she whispered. "This young man belongs to your mother, too. She deserves to share this time with us."

"I love you, Mrs. Parrish." Jeff bent down and kissed her, long and tenderly. The girls watched, beaming like little Cheshire cats.

"I'm going to write stories for the baby," Flannery announced, "and as soon as he's big enough to listen, I'll read them all to him."

"I'll draw him pictures," Ellen said. "And I'll teach him to play chess—if he doesn't eat the chess pieces."

"Do you know what I wish?" Kate gazed at each of their faces, her love all but spilling over into tears.

"What?" Flannery asked.

"I wish that I had great big six-foot arms like a mother gorilla, so I could hug all of you at the same time!"

"That's all right," said Ellen. "We can all hug *you*."

And that's just what they did.

* * * * *

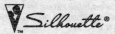

Take 4 bestselling love stories FREE

Plus get a FREE surprise gift!

Special Limited-time Offer

Mail to Silhouette Reader Service™

3010 Walden Avenue
P.O. Box 1867
Buffalo, N.Y. 14240-1867

YES! Please send me 4 free Silhouette Romance™ novels and my free surprise gift. Then send me 6 brand-new novels every month, which I will receive months before they appear in bookstores. Bill me at the low price of $2.67 each plus 25¢ delivery and applicable sales tax, if any.* That's the complete price and a savings of over 10% off the cover prices—quite a bargain! I understand that accepting the books and gift places me under no obligation ever to buy any books. I can always return a shipment and cancel at any time. Even if I never buy another book from Silhouette, the 4 free books and the surprise gift are mine to keep forever.

215 BPA A3UT

Name _____ (PLEASE PRINT)

Address _____ Apt. No. _____

City _____ State _____ Zip _____

This offer is limited to one order per household and not valid to present Silhouette Romance™ subscribers. *Terms and prices are subject to change without notice. Sales tax applicable in N.Y.

USROM-696   ©1990 Harlequin Enterprises Limited

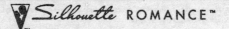

You've been waiting for him all your life....
Now your Prince has finally arrived!

In fact, *three* handsome princes
are coming your way in

ROYAL WEDDINGS

A delightful new miniseries by **LISA KAYE LAUREL**
about three bachelor princes who find happily-ever-
after with three small-town women!

Coming in September 1997—THE PRINCE'S BRIDE

Crown Prince Erik Anders would do anything for his
country—even plan a pretend marriage to his lovely
castle caretaker. But could he convince the king, and
the rest of the world, that his proposal was real—before
his cool heart melted for his small-town "bride"?

Coming in November 1997—THE PRINCE'S BABY

Irresistible Prince Whit Anders was shocked to
discover that the summer romance he'd had years
ago had resulted in a very royal baby! Now that
pretty Drew Davis's secret was out, could her kiss
turn the sexy prince into a full-time dad?

**Look for prince number three in the exciting
conclusion to ROYAL WEDDINGS,
coming in 1998—only from**

Silhouette ROMANCE™

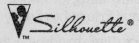